"I don't know how you got here or what we've been doing—I'm just very grateful."

Bryan's breath whispered on her neck as he reached out to caress her shoulder.

"We haven't been doing anything—except sleeping." Finley pulled the bathrobe close and inched from him. His arm shot out to wrap about her waist. "Stop it! You're ill and you shouldn't be—"

His mouth covered hers in a hard, quick kiss. "Who's ill? Me?" Again his lips captured hers and this time stayed to taste and tease. His arm tightened about her waist, and he pulled her to him.

Finley squirmed for a moment, but his mouth was too intoxicating and she ceased her struggling. A flowering warmth grew in her stomach to blossom down her legs, and she pressed closer to him. He was like wildfire, and the feel of him sent the rest of the world into a void, leaving only the touch, taste, and smell of him.

"Finley, I'm so glad you're here . . . so glad . . ."

TOMORROW'S BRIDE

by Delaine Tucker

A WALLABY BOOK

PUBLISHED BY SIMON & SCHUSTER

NEW YORK

This novel is a work of fiction. Names, characters, places and incidents are either the product of the author's imagination or are used fictitiously. Any resemblance to actual events or locales, or persons, living or dead, is entirely coincidental.

Text copyright © 1982 by Delaine Tucker
Illustrations copyright © 1982 by Eric Maché
All rights reserved
including the right of reproduction
in whole or in part in any form
Published by Wallaby Books
A Simon & Schuster Division of
Gulf & Western Corporation
Simon & Schuster Building
1230 Avenue of the Americas
New York, New York 10020

SERENADE and design are trademarks
of Simon & Schuster

WALLABY and colophon are registered
trademarks of Simon & Schuster

First Wallaby Books Printing January 1982
10 9 8 7 6 5 4 3 2 1
Manufactured in the United States of America

Library of Congress Catalog Card Number: 81-69966

ISBN 0-671-44359-3

To the Tulsa Night Writers,
Oklahoma's finest

1

The artificial turf crunched beneath Finley Malone's tennis shoes as she walked toward the long bench positioned near the sidelines. Finley hitched her camera case strap higher on her shoulder and listened to the grunts and thuds of the men who were engaged in one-on-one football drills.

As she neared the bench, Finley raised her hand in greeting. "Hi, Dad. I'm reporting for duty."

Mike "The Hammer" Malone gave her a broad grin. He pulled the green and gold cap from his head and wiped his brow with the back of his burly hand. "Finley! Just on time!" He kissed her cheek. "Got your camera, have you? Well, you just make yourself at home. Take some pictures of this practice, if you want." He gave her a swift hug. "I gotta watch these luggers. Okay?"

"Sure, Dad. Don't worry about me. I'll just get my footing around here." Finley sat on the bench and set the camera case at her side. She glanced up at the sun and decided the temperature had already soared past eighty degrees. Summer was making a last stand before giving way to the cool breezes of fall.

Finley shifted on the hard bench and watched the football players. It was their first day in full uniform and pads and they were sweating under the strong rays of the sun. They'd been practicing since midsummer, and now that September was here they could sense the official beginning of football season. Another two or three weeks and the air would be brisk instead of sultry and the trees in Tulsa would dress themselves in autumn gold and yellow.

"Hi!"

Finley looked to her right to see a lovely woman approaching her. The woman flashed Finley a friendly smile.

"I'm Gena Jackson. Are you a wife or a girlfriend?" She held out her hand to Finley.

"I'm a daughter." Finley shook the extended hand and smiled at the woman's puzzlement.

"A daughter?" Gena placed her hands on her slim hips and glanced around at the struggling football players. "Which one of them is your dad?"

Finley laughed. "Mike Malone is my dad."

Gena turned back to her. "You're Finley? I'm glad to meet you. Mike talks about you all the time."

"Are you Jilly Jackson's wife?"

"In the flesh." Gena sat beside Finley and eyed the camera case. "So, you're going to be the team photographer this season?"

Finley nodded. "One of them. Frank Benson is still the number one photographer. Dad's letting me travel with the team this year so I can get pictures for my portfolio."

"You graduated from college this year, didn't you?"

"Yes. Now, I'm facing the cold, cruel world of employment."

Gena laughed. "I don't envy you. I've been through that myself."

"What did you do? I mean, what profession?"

"I was a model before I married Jilly. Now, I'm a football widow."

Finley examined the woman's perfect complexion, refined features, and correct posture. "I should have known. You're beautiful. Just the way a model should look."

Gena smiled. "Thank you. Are you looking forward to this job?"

"Oh, yes. It's not really a job—just an internship. I'm kind of leery about the whole thing . . ." Finley let her voice trail off as she fished her camera from the leather case.

"Because your father is head coach of the team?" Gena asked.

"Yes." Finley shook her head. "Seems like favoritism, doesn't it?"

"Well, in any job, knowing the right people is important. But that only gets you the job—your talent is the reason you keep it."

"You're right, I guess. I hope everybody sees it that way." Finley lifted the 35mm camera and peered through the lens.

"Don't worry about what everybody thinks, hon. You just do your thing and have fun. Ooooops!" Gena laughed. "Jilly just took a solid hit."

Finley found the fallen player in the camera lens and snapped the shutter. "He's okay. He's getting up."

"Sure he is. It takes a tank to get Jilly down for good." Gena's tone held a measure of pride.

"I've always liked Jilly."

"Oh yeah! I forgot that you've been practically raised around these guys. They're like family, aren't they?"

Finley lowered the camera. "Some of them. Really, I barely know most of the guys. I've been in college and even when I'm around, I see them, but I hardly ever get to talk to any of them. Jilly's different." Finley looked at Gena. "Jilly's always so friendly."

Gena nodded, her gaze still on her husband. "Jilly *loves* people."

A shrill whistle sounded and the players ground to a halt. Mike Malone lifted a megaphone to his mouth and shouted, "Okay, let's take a break, then I want to see the defensive line and the offense can work on the tires."

Finley watched Jilly lumber toward them. The big black man smiled when he spied his wife and Finley.

"Hey, honey!" He placed a kiss on Gena's cheek. "What's the occasion? Hi, Finley."

Gena made room on the bench for Jilly. "Oh, I had some

time to kill so I thought I'd drop by and watch some of the practice. Finley took a picture of you while you were sprawled out on the turf."

Jilly frowned. "Finley! Why not wait until I make a sensational catch in the end zone and then take your pictures? Give old Jilly a break, okay?"

Finley laughed. "I was just fooling around. I'll get plenty of pictures of you scoring this season. Don't worry." Finley gazed across the playing field where a movement attracted her attention. She squinted against the sun to focus on ten girls clad in green and gold outfits. "Who are they?"

Jilly followed Finley's pointing finger. "Those are our cheerleaders. How do those outfits grab you, Gena?"

Gena scowled. "Not much to them."

Finley nodded in agreement as she examined the short, pleated skirts of green and gold and the shimmering, gold halter tops. "I didn't know we had cheerleaders."

Jilly chuckled. "Don't imagine your dad would talk about them much. The manager and owners decided we need cheerleaders since we might get to the Super Bowl this year. Coach Malone isn't crazy about the idea. He thinks it's hogwash."

Finley laughed. "That sounds like Dad. He probably thinks they'll interfere with his team."

"Right," Jilly said with a grin. "The coach tried to push through a rule that forbids the cheerleaders from dating the players, but the management nixed it. Coach Malone is miffed because one of the girls is dating Bryan."

"Bryan Brady?" Finley asked as her mind projected a picture of the team's quarterback.

"Yeah. He's dating the head cheerleader. The girl there in the middle." Jilly pointed across the field.

Finley examined the shapely blonde who was posing for pictures for Frank Benson. The girl's high-pitched giggle floated across the field to Finley.

Jilly laughed. "Of course, I don't think she's anything serious to Bryan. He keeps things pretty loose."

Finley raised an eyebrow. "How true! Everything I've read or heard about him leads me to believe that he sees women as mindless playthings put on earth just for his amusement."

Jilly laughed and elbowed Gena. "Listen to that, will you? Finley's got quite a sharp tongue. I'd better stay on her good side." He sobered and focused his attention past his wife. "Speak of the devil."

Finley tensed and looked to her right to see Number Ten walking toward them. An ironic smile touched Finley's lips. *This* is a perfect ten? She shook her head. Not in *my* book. He's as well known for his conceit and arrogance as for his playing. Shouldn't think like that, she scolded herself, considering you've never even met him! Give him the benefit of the doubt.

As Bryan Brady neared them, he pulled his green and gold helmet from his head. Sunlight caught at the red highlights in his sandy hair and Finley noted that his hair had a tendency to curl—especially now that it was wet with perspiration. Cobalt blue eyes glinted as his gaze brushed over Finley before finding Jilly. Brady grinned.

"Hey, Jilly! I like your bookends." He winked at Gena. "Hi, Gena. Long time no see."

"And whose fault is that, Bryan?" Gena asked as Brady sat next to her. "We invited you to dinner twice and you always had a previous engagement. I think you're busier in the off-season than you are during the season."

Brady laughed. "You're right. I had those youth football camps to conduct this summer and in the evenings I craved *adult* companionship." His eyes twinkled, then shifted to find Finley again. "Do I know you?"

"You ought to know her, Bryan," Jilly said. "This is Mike's daughter, Finley."

"Well, well." He allowed his gaze to rest on Finley's face for a few seconds before it swept her figure. "You're Mike's daughter, huh? Our unofficial photographer?"

Finley tensed under the cool appraisal of his eyes. His gaze moved lazily over her mass of auburn curls to stare unwaveringly into her green eyes. She fought the sudden impulse to look away from him, knowing that he would take that as a sign of shyness. Instead, she straightened her back and stared at him boldly as his gaze moved to encompass her small, shapely frame. When his cobalt eyes moved to the slight dimple in her chin, he smiled.

Vaguely, Finley wondered if he approved of what he saw or if he was disappointed. The thought sent a wave of anger coursing through her. With a start, she noticed his cocked eyebrow and she realized that he was waiting for a response to his question. Finley lifted her chin and felt resentment curl inside her.

How dare he stare at her so openly as if she were here on display just for him! She narrowed her green eyes and cleared her throat.

"Intern photographer," Finley corrected in a terse tone. "Nice to meet you."

He nodded, then rolled his shoulders as if uncoiling a set of tight muscles. "I hate to break up the party, but it's back to work, Jilly." Brady swung his helmet by the chin strap. "Nice to meet you, kid."

Finley fumed. Kid! She glared at him and swallowed her anger as she watched him saunter toward the white tires. Jilly patted Gena's hand and then scampered after Brady.

"Ooooo! What an obnoxious man!"

Gena glanced at Finley. "Which one?"

"Brady, of course!" Finley watched Brady prance nimbly through the center of the tires with an easy, athletic grace.

"Oh, he's not so bad once you get used to him," Gena said.

"Did you hear what he called me? He called me 'kid.' The creep!"

Gena laughed. "He calls everybody that! Don't take it so personally, Finley."

"Well, I hope I don't have to deal with him very much. My instincts are good, and they tell me that he's a first-class louse."

"Finley, you'd better prepare yourself for the worst. After all, he *is* the quarterback, so I imagine you'll be around him quite a bit."

Finley sighed. "I'll let Frank worry about the pictures of the quarterback."

"I don't see how your portfolio will be complete without pictures of Bryan passing or handing off the ball," Gena noted in a quiet voice.

Finley frowned. "You're right." She shrugged. "I'll use my telephoto lens when I shoot him so I can keep at a safe distance."

"I know the real problem," Gena said with a giggle. "It's two Irish personalities clashing." She laughed. "Hey, why not put that camera away for a couple of hours and join me for lunch?"

Finley grinned. "Great idea." She glanced at Brady again. "Maybe you're right, Gena. I've never really been around an Irishman before—except for my dad. It might not be healthy for me." Finley placed her camera in the case, snapped the case shut, and slung it onto her shoulder. "I'm ready and I'm starving."

Gena drove to a quiet restaurant in Tulsa, just a few minutes from the practice field. The restaurant owner knew Gena and escorted them to a table near a window.

Finley ordered French onion soup and a club sandwich. Finley tasted the soup. "Mmmm! This is great."

Gena leaned toward her. "That's the best French onion soup in Oklahoma—without a doubt."

"It *is* the best I've tasted." Finley spooned more of the tangy soup into her mouth.

"I guess your dad's glad you'll be traveling with him this season, huh?"

Finley sighed. "Dad doesn't know anyone's around during

football season. He won't even notice me." Finley smiled. "I'm used to it, and I'll probably be just as bad once I get into this work. Put a camera in front of my face and everything else fades far into the background."

"What are your career plans, Finley?"

"Oh, I'd like to be a free-lance sports photographer or maybe get on with one of the sports magazines. It's a very competitive business."

"I'll bet. A lot like fashion modeling in that respect."

Finley examined Gena for a few moments, then snapped her fingers. "Now I'm able to place you! You've been on the cover of lots of magazines, but I particularly remember the photo on the front of *Charisma* magazine. Hey, didn't you win some kind of award?"

Gena laughed. "Not an award, just a list. The fashion photographers voted me 1978's most popular black model."

"Of course! Well, they have excellent taste. I'd love to have the sophisticated look of a model."

Gena pursed her shapely lips. "You have that fresh, youthful look that's so popular today. Don't knock it."

"Yeah, I look like a teenager most of the time. I'm working on looking older."

Gena shook her head and her black hair brushed the tops of her shoulders. "Don't rush it! Didn't you know that youth is in?" She scrutinized Finley for a few moments. "You have what the model agencies call an 'elfin' face. If it weren't for that auburn hair, you could pass yourself off as French."

"French?" Finley laughed. "Me? Ha! I'm Irish-American, through and through. I even believe in leprechauns."

Gena laughed and then sipped her coffee in thoughtful silence. "Who styled your hair, Finley?"

Finley patted her short, curly locks. "Me. Why? What's wrong?"

"Nothing! I was just thinking how attractive the hairstyle is on you. Of course, you have just the right face for it. Short hair goes well with heart-shaped faces, and that style shows off your green eyes, too. Don't change a thing."

Finley nodded. "To tell you the truth, I keep my hair like this because the style is easy to take care of. I'm terrible with fancy hairstyles and fancy makeup. I've never gotten the hang of it."

"I heard that your father raised you."

"Yes. Mother died when I was four. Lucky for Dad that I was a tomboy."

Gena giggled. "Got a steady boyfriend?"

"No, not anymore. We—well, we broke up right before school ended. Keith wanted me to give up my ideas about photography and run off to Maine with him and work in his father's business—an insurance company. We just didn't see eye to eye, I guess."

"You don't sound brokenhearted," Gena observed.

"No. It wasn't that serious." Finley changed the subject. "Are you going to travel with the team?"

Gena shook her head. "No way. You know how your father is during the season? Well, Jilly is the same. I'll just stay here."

"It must have been hard at first—getting used to Jilly's obsession with football, I mean."

Gena finished her coffee before she answered. "It was at first, but I'm used to it now. We've been married for five years, and I've learned to be by myself until after the New Year—then, I've got Jilly all to myself again."

"Do you have children?"

"No," Gena answered, then smiled. "But we're working on it. Are you ready to leave?"

"Yes. Could you drop me back at the practice field?"

"Sure. No problem."

Gena and Finley paid their bills, and as Gena drove back to the practice field, Finley took in the passing scenery. It was great to be back in Tulsa—so clean and fresh in the summer. Soon she spotted the University of Tulsa with its vine-covered buildings. At the field, Finley said good-bye to Gena and then strolled toward the field.

At the end of the football field, she watched the various groups of players practice their moves, passes, and receptions. Idly, she lifted her camera and focused on the crossbar overhead. A bird flew into view and she adjusted her lens quickly and snapped the shutter. That won't turn out, she thought, then shrugged. Something else flew into her camera's viewfinder and she focused. A football! A split second passed before it occured to her that the ball was getting larger and larger.

"Hey, kid!"

Fingers dug into the flesh of her upper arm and she was jerked to one side. She stumbled, and arms stole around her waist for support. Finley gasped when Bryan Brady's face appeared before her.

"Let go of me!" Finley wrenched from his embrace and gave him a murderous glare. "What's with you?"

He placed his hands on his narrow hips and nodded at a spot on the ground. "You almost got beaned, kid. Were you napping or what?"

Finley looked at the ground beside her and spotted the football. What was I thinking about? she wondered. She shook her head, then looked at Brady again. He was grinning.

"I don't like to be called kid. My name is Finley."

He raised his eyebrows. "Oh, excuse me! I didn't mean to insult you. I call—"

"I know. You call everyone kid. I just don't like it." Finley checked her camera to make sure nothing was broken, then turned on her heel and stalked away from him.

"Hey, Finley!"

She stopped and glanced over her shoulder. "Yes?"

"Aren't you going to thank me? Didn't the coach teach you any manners?"

Finley's attention was arrested by Kevin Rogers. The lithe athlete was running backward toward Brady. Finley flinched, certain that Rogers would plow into Brady. However, Rogers stopped inches from the quarterback and caught a football that was spinning toward Brady. Roger turned and looked from Brady to Finley. Amusement flitted over his dark face.

Finley cleared her throat. "Thanks, Mister Brady."

"*Mister* Brady?!" Rogers hooted. "Hey, Finley, how come you never call me mister? Brady's just another football player like me."

Finley frowned when she saw Brady's taunting smile. "We're friends, Kevin. I don't call friends mister."

"Oh, okay. That explains it." Kevin slapped Brady on the back. "Tough luck, Brady." He laughed and ran toward the sidelines.

Brady's smile diminished somewhat. "You know, Finley, I should have let that ball pop right on top of that red head of yours. What have you got against me, anyway?"

Finley squared her shoulders and turned to face him. "Nothing, really. I just don't like your attitude toward me. I'm not a—"

He cut her off. "Listen, little lady." He strode toward her. "If you think I'm going to treat you special just because you're Mike Malone's daughter, then think again. You're just another dame to me. Got it?"

Finley raised her chin so that she could look him in the eye. She found it impossible since he was at least a foot taller than she. "I've got it. And you're nothing but another jock to me. Got it?"

He narrowed his eyes, and Finley saw the stern set of his jaw. "You're not going to be too welcome around here if you call the guys on the team that."

Finley smiled. "I don't intend to call them that. I save that particular noun for when it's appropriate. You're the first specimen I've found. Excuse me." She whirled from him and walked briskly to the sidelines. Her heart was pounding against her rib cage and she half expected him to follow her.

"Hey, Brady! Catch!"

Finley turned to find that Brady was where she'd left him. A football was sailing toward him, and he turned and caught it. He gave her one last biting glance before he cocked his arm and sent the ball spiraling toward Jilly. Finley was relieved when Brady moved to join the others at practice.

Frank Benson ambled toward her. Four cameras swung from straps about his neck and shoulders. "Hi, cutie. I've got something for you." He handed Finley a black notebook. "Those are this year's team pictures. You'll need to memorize the numbers and the faces they belong to. Okay?"

Finley nodded and watched as Frank tore the wrapper from a candy bar and quickly devoured the whole thing. You sure don't need that, Frank, she thought as she examined his round waist and double chins.

Frank laughed. "I know! I've seen that look before. My wife is the champ at it." He patted his stomach. "The doctor told me to watch my weight, so I'm getting it out here so I can watch it!" He chuckled at his joke. "Finley, I've got me a powerful sweet tooth. I fought it for years, but it won a few years ago. I'm a good loser, I guess."

Finley smiled. "Okay, Frank, no more scolding looks from me. We all have our vices." She sat on the artificial grass. "I'll look these over. I know most of the guys, so I should be able to memorize this in no time."

"Okay, cutie. Well, I guess I'll get some shots of Bryan now. 'Bye." He waddled from her toward Number Ten.

Brady! Finley frowned and opened the book. Bryan Brady smiled at her. She closed the book for a moment, then opened it again. He was still there.

Resigned to the fact that she couldn't seem to escape him, Finley examined the color photograph. His sandy hair fell in rings on his forehead and curled at his neck. There didn't seem to be any particular style to it, Finley decided. He just let his hair fall where it wanted. Kind of attractive, she thought, then steeled herself against such insanity. His dark blue eyes were framed with black lashes that were thick and spiky. His nose looked as if it had been broken once or twice, and his mouth was curved into that lopsided smile he seemed to use as a weapon. She noted how the thin upper lip contrasted seductively with the full lower one and a tiny, faded scar at the left corner of his mouth added to the off-center grin, Heavens! He looks ornery! she thought. He had a square, typically Irish jaw that spoke of a long line of stubborn, thick-skinned ancestors.

Finley read the statistics that were typed neatly below his picture.

"Brady, Bryan. QB. Notre Dame." Naturally, the Fighting Irish. What else? "5-10-1950." Taurus. Bull-headed, of course. "Boston, Mass., 6'2", 190 lbs. Joined the Tulsa Wildcatters in 1972 as a first-draft choice. Became first-string quarterback in 1977. Heisman Trophy runner-up." Tough luck, Brady. The best man won, I guess.

Finley closed the book. They don't mention that he's a first-class jerk who loves to talk about all the ladies in his life. Finley fumed as she recalled the magazine articles she'd read about him. Male chauvinist! Her temperature soared when she remembered all the pictures she'd seen in gossip magazines. Brady dating socialites. Brady dumping socialites. Brady dating actresses. Brady dumping actresses. Brady dating married women. Brady dumping married women. Why doesn't someone dump *him* for a change?

A smile touched her mouth. Now, that would be fun! Dumping the Great Number Ten right on his compact rump! Finley giggled. Surely, *that* would make headlines!

"Hey, Finley! Are you going to sit there all day or are you going to take pictures?"

Finley blinked away the vision and looked up at Frank.

"Oh, Frank!" She scurried to her feet. "Sorry. I was just thinking—"

"Do that later, okay? Let's get some film shot."

"Right, Frank." Finley placed the book beside her other things and picked up her camera. She spotted Brady on the south side of the field and she headed north.

2

The powder room was empty, and Finley was glad to be alone for a few minutes. She sat before the mirror and breathed in the silence. She glanced at the powder room door.

It's so noisy out there, she thought. I can hear the din even in here. Oh well! What do you expect from football players who are celebrating the coming season?

She took her compact from her purse and tried vainly to cover the freckles that sprinkled her nose. Useless! She sighed as she removed her lipstick from her purse and lined her mouth with a peach color that matched her evening gown. Pushing the compact and lipstick back into her purse, Finley stood and surveyed her image. She smothered a giggle as she recalled her father's shocked expression when he'd seen the daring evening gown. Your little girl's grown up, Dad, she thought as she examined the way the sparkling peach-colored gown hugged her curves.

Finley turned and glanced over her bare shoulder at the way the back of the dress dipped dangerously below her waist.

"Oooo, Finley! You're so naughty!" Finley told her image.

Something moved in the mirror, and Finley glanced up to see a sequined blonde. She smiled and tried to hide her embarrassment.

"Oh, hello."

"Hi." The blonde moved to sit in one of the small chairs in front of the mirror.

Finley studied her for a moment. "Aren't you one of the cheerleaders?"

"Yes." The woman's brown eyes focused on Finley. "You're Malone's kid, right?"

Finley chewed on her lower lip, then answered evenly, "I'm Finley Malone." The word "kid" stuck in her mind, and then she remembered. This was the cheerleader Bryan Brady was seeing!

"Pleased to meet you. I'm Kristi Sinclair." She laughed suddenly, then hiccuped. "Ooops!" Her brown eyes twinkled. "Bryan told me about you almost getting whopped in the head by a football. Good thing he saved you!"

Finley flexed her fingers and wished she could wrap them around Brady's neck. "He exaggerated, which I'm sure he does quite often. He didn't save my life."

Kristi shrugged her small shoulders. "Say, do you have a cigarette, honey?"

"No, I don't." Finley turned to leave.

"Hey, how do you like your new job?"

Finley turned back to the woman. "It's challenging." She watched as Kristi patted her blond hair into place, and noticed the trace of black roots where her hair parted.

"It's nice that your dad gave you a break. You know, when I tried out for cheerleader there were over a hundred girls there. Wasn't anybody there to give me a hand. I had to rely on my talent." She straightened her spine so that her breasts lifted, then smiled in the mirror at Finley.

Finley glared at the blonde, then turned back to wrench open the door. "Well, rah rah for you. Bye!" Anger blocked her vision for a moment, and she sucked in her breath when her body collided with a solid form.

"Hi. Is Kristi in there?"

Finley took a step backward and stared up at Bryan Brady. "Uh—yes! Would you like me to get her for you?"

Brady smiled and Finley noticed the tiny lines that crinkled the skin at the corners of his eyes. "No. That's okay. Would you like to call a truce and dance with me?"

Finley examined him carefully and saw no ulterior motives lurking in his splintery blue eyes. "Okay." She shrugged and preceded him to the dance floor.

Her ears caught the slow beat of a ballad and Finley tensed when she felt the warmth of Brady's arms circle her waist. His touch, while compelling, seemed impersonal, and Finley lifted her lashes to lock with his gaze. Mild curiosity was evident there, but that was all.

"Are you dropping out of school this year to travel with the team?" he asked in a near whisper.

"School?" Finley drew back a little. "I've graduated."

"What?" He blinked. "No, I mean college."

Finley bobbed her head. "Right. So do I."

Now, it was he who drew back. "You've graduated from college?! What are you—a whiz kid? How old are you?"

Finley sighed her irritation. "I'm twenty-one."

Disbelief shadowed his face for an instant. "Twenty-one?" He looked toward the ladies' powder room. "But, Kristi is—"

Finley nodded. "She's twenty-one, too. I know."

Brady examined her for a moment. "But Kristi looks so much older than you."

Finley felt a smirk twist her lips. "Well, that's the price you pay for experience, I guess."

His eyes widened, then narrowed quickly. Finley watched the play of his tongue along the inside of his mouth and she wondered what he was thinking. She felt the splay of his fingers and the warmth of his palm at her back and her heart triphammered.

"Well, well. That changes things, doesn't it? I thought you were jailbait. You're legal!" His voice was a purr.

Instinctively, Finley stiffened her spine when his large hand pressed her to him. His lips touched the top of her ear.

"Hey!" She wiggled against the firm strength of his chest. "Cut it out, will you? Quit acting like a delinquent."

"We're both too old to be delinquents, Finley," he whispered and his breath played with the hair near her ear. "The coach talks about you as if you were a teenybopper. He had me fooled."

"To Dad, I *am* a teenybopper." Finley turned her head so that his lips were no longer caressing her ear. "I asked you to stop!"

"Stop? The song isn't over yet." His lips grazed her cheek in a sliding kiss.

Finley raised her foot and brought her spiked heel down squarely on his leather shoe. She couldn't prevent the grin from spreading across her lips when she saw him wince and add an inch of space between their bodies. He kept his hand on her back and gripped her hand tightly.

"Now who's being a delinquent, Finley?"

Before she could fling a retort at him, Brady pulled her to him and with light, fast steps moved her across the dance floor. Finley blinked and struggled for balance. Cool air touched her heated skin, and she gasped when she found herself out on the club's terrace.

"What are you—" She smothered back the rest of her complaint as Brady gripped her hand tighter and whirled her about before setting her free. Finley stumbled, then gained her balance.

Fury seized her when she spotted his amused expression. Snapping her jaws shut, she marched toward the sliding glass doors that gave entrance to the club. Brady stepped sideways to block her escape.

"Move!" Finley snapped at him and gave him a killing glare.

He seemed not to notice. "Afraid your daddy will miss you?"

"I agreed to dance with you. I didn't agree to stand out here on the terrace with you. Now, move out of my way!" Finley placed a shoulder against him and tried to shove his imposing body to one side. His fingers curved about her shoulders and he laughed.

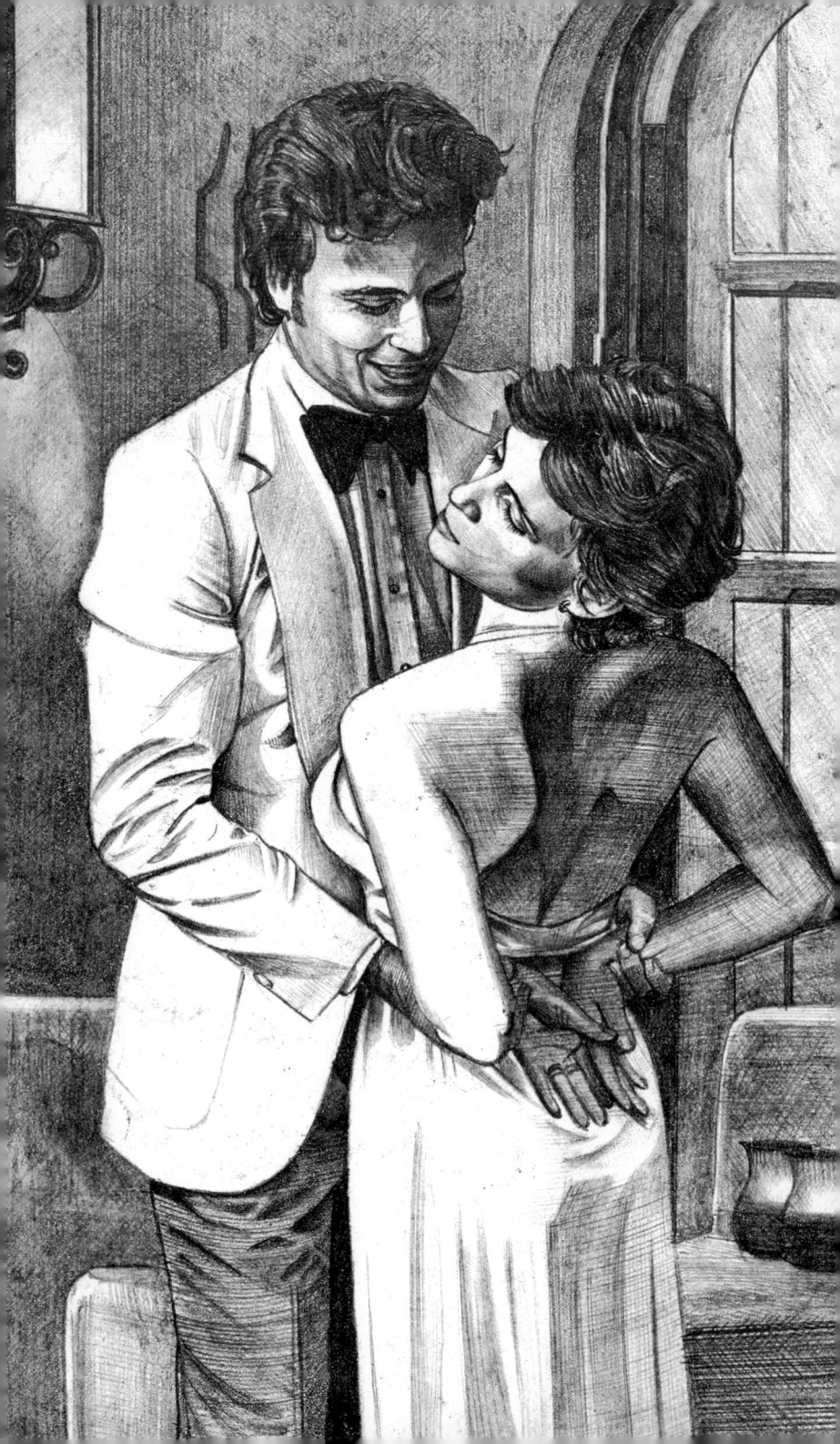

"So, you want to dance? Okay. Let's dance." His hands slid down her arms to catch her hands and he bent her arms back so that they were trapped behind her. She found herself fitted against him as he began to move to the faint tune. His eyes laughed down into hers. "Nice, huh?"

Her anger was so intense that Finley wondered if she were capable of spitting fireballs at him. A sixth sense told her that anger would be a reward to him, so she lifted her chin and curbed her lashing tongue.

"You think you're cute, don't you?" she asked in a quiet voice.

He grinned. "I *know* I'm cute. And more."

"How about immature, a fluffy-headed jock who never mentally graduated from high school? I mean, look at yourself! You're the quarterback and you're *still* going steady with the head cheerleader. You're pitiful."

The amused warmth left his eyes and a cold, hard look replaced it. The expression froze Finley's tongue. She felt herself flinch from the frost as he pushed her from him.

"What's with you?" His voice was like flint sparking against her nerve endings. "I'm just having a little fun!" He ran the fingers of one hand through his hair and tossed her an angry look. "Am I bleeding? I should be from that tongue-lashing!"

A swishing sound behind her forced Finley to tear her gaze from his face to stare at Kristi Sinclair. The blonde gave Finley a vehement glance before gliding toward Brady. Kristi tucked her hand in the crook of Brady's arm, and Finley found herself noting the contrast of the woman's tanned skin against Brady's white dinner jacket.

"What's going on out here?" Kristi didn't bother to hide the suspicion from her voice.

Brady shook his head, but kept his gaze on Finley. "Oh, nothing. I was trying to seduce the coach's daughter, but you've loused it up."

Kristi stared at him, her gaze darting to his eyes, his

mouth, his chin, then back to his eyes as if she were searching for a disclaimer there.

The tense silence shook Finley from her suspended state and she managed a shaky laugh. "He's joking, Kristi. Believe me, he's joking. It was stuffy in there, so we just—just—"

"Stepped out here to do a little heavy breathing," Brady finished smoothly and grinned.

His words knocked the breath from Finley for a moment and she found herself staring at him, dumbfounded. "No!" Finley shook her head again. "N-no. Quit teasing, Brady," she pleaded with him.

A sandy eyebrow climbed his forehead. "Oh." He sobered and nodded with grave intent. "Okay, I've got the game plan now." He covered Kristi's hand with his own. "Let's join the party, Kristi, honey." He guided Kristi to the sliding door.

Gratefully, Finley turned and pushed back the door. She stepped over the threshold just as she felt Brady's breath on the back of her neck.

"You don't like to kiss-and-tell, right?" His whisper was pitched just loud enough, for Kristi's benefit.

Finley whirled to face him and encountered Kristi's jealous stare. Brady was smiling. Finley threw up her hands in surrender. "I give! I give! Now leave me alone. Go bother someone else." She frowned at him, then hurried to join the others at the long dining table.

As Finley sat at the table, she caught her father's narrowed glare, but she chose to ignore it.

"Been practicing your moves, Bryan?" Riley Thompson, a running back, grinned at Brady.

Brady glanced at Mike Malone before he answered Thompson. "No. The coach's daughter was just giving me a few pointers."

Thompson threw back his head and laughed and the others at the table joined him. Finley shifted her gaze from her empty plate to her father's murderous expression.

She winced. I'm going to catch it tonight when I get home, she thought. Thanks, Brady. Thanks a lot.

"I knew it! I knew it!" Mike Malone threw himself onto the living room sofa and pointed an accusing finger at Finley. "Didn't I tell you this would happen? Didn't I?" He didn't wait for an answer. "The guys are already rubbing it in, getting under my skin over you. What were you doing with Bryan, anyway?"

"Nothing!" Finley collapsed in the armchair and sighed. "Give me some credit, Dad. I hate Brady! If I was going to take up with someone on the team, he'd be my last choice."

"Don't you take up with *anybody* on the team!" Mike wagged a warning, stubby finger. "I don't want you hooked up with a football player. Understand?"

Finley rolled her eyes heavenward. "We've been through this and through this."

"And we're going through it again until you get it through your skull. No football players!"

"I don't understand you!" Finley raised her voice to stop his rejoinder. "*You're* a former football player and you've raised me around football players and—"

"I did that so you'd see what kind of life they lead. I want you to marry a doctor or teacher or lawyer. Not an athlete."

Finley leaned forward. "What's wrong with them?"

"What's wrong with them?!" Her father looked at her as if she'd lost her mind. "They travel all the time—never home when you need them—they chase skirts constantly and they—they—"

"They make good livings and they have great bodies," Finley finished and flashed him a teasing smile.

Her father measured her with a comprehensive glance. "Bodies? Bodies! You just keep your eyes off their bodies."

Finley doubled over in laughter. When she finally regained her composure, she wiped the tears from her eyes and shook her head at her father's thunderous face. "Oh, Dad! Sometimes you're so cute. Listen, you know how the guys are! They're full of hot air. They're just kidding you. Let it roll off your shoulders and they'll quit."

Some of the storm signals left her father's face, and he took a deep breath that expanded his broad chest. When he spoke, his voice was soft and lilting. "Finley, girl, the trouble is, I love you. I don't like the guys kidding about you. It's not funny to me."

Finley felt new tears film her eyes, and she rose from the chair and sat next to her father. "Oh, Daddy!" She buried her face in the sleeve of his dinner jacket. "I love you, too. But, let me handle myself now. Okay? I'm all grown up!"

Mike Malone caressed Finley's cheek and sighed. "I wish your mother was here. She'd know whether or not I'm overreacting. I just don't want to see you hurt. I want you to marry some nice guy who'll give you a house with a white picket fence around it."

Finley smiled. "Maybe I don't want that kind of life, Dad. Have you ever thought about that?"

"Well, no. What kind of life *do* you want?"

Finley furrowed her brow. "Something out of the ordinary. I don't want my life to be routine." She raised her head and examined her father's confused expression. "Dad, if I'd wanted the safe, mundane kind of life-style I could have had that with Keith."

Mike nodded his head. "Okay, little one. I'll try to keep my big, ugly nose out of your business. Just watch those guys on the team. They're a bunch of clowns."

"Especially Brady," Finley said as she stood.

"He's no worse than the rest of them." Mike stretched and yawned. "Well we'd better call it a day. Sleep well."

Finley placed a kiss on her father's forehead. "I love you, Dad. Good night."

She turned and went to her bedroom. The evening seemed

to have drained her of energy, and by the time she had showered and dressed for bed, Finley felt exhausted. With a sigh, she relaxed on the bed and stared at the ceiling. Her thoughts returned to the party, and she saw Bryan Brady's mischievous grin and laughing eyes.

He's going to be difficult to work around, she thought. He loves to play with people. Loves to embarrass them. Finley turned onto her side and closed her eyes. I'll just ignore him, she mused. I'll pretend he doesn't exist.

The office door opened and Bryan Brady stepped into the corridor. Finley moved farther down the hall into the shadows, dreading any confrontation with the team's quarterback.

"Hey, Bryan!"

Brady turned to greet Riley Thompson. "Hey, old buddy, what's up?"

"We're heading for the Wildcat Club to have a few drinks with the guys who got cut from the team today. You know, a kind of 'sorry to see you go and good luck' party. They sent me to find you."

Finley held her breath, not daring to move for fear Brady would see her. She watched, fascinated, as regret colored his expression.

"Yeah, I'll come with you. How many got cut today?"

"About a dozen, I think." Riley ran a hand through his hair. "Tough luck."

"Yes, it is."

"Hey!" Riley's mood brightened and he grinned. "There's someone waiting for you at the club."

"Oh? Who?"

"That redheaded stewardess—what's her name?"

Brady grinned. "Sweet Sonja."

"Right!" Riley slapped him on the back. "She's in town and she is looking for you. I told her to meet us at the club.

How do you juggle all these women, Bryan?"

Brady shrugged and a cunning smile captured his mouth. "It takes practice, my boy. Lots of practice."

Riley opened his mouth to respond to Brady's kidding remark, then froze as his gaze rested on the shadows where Finley stood. Surprised at Riley's expression, Brady whirled to face Finley.

Finley sighed and walked toward them, trying to appear cool and confident and strictly business.

"Hello, Riley, Brady."

Brady smiled and bowed slightly. "Eavesdropping, Miss Malone?"

"Certainly not!" Finley felt her cheeks flush with her lie. "I—I'm here to see—to see Frank. I'm supposed to meet him in Dad's office." She eyed the door that was blocked by Brady. "Excuse me?"

Brady chuckled and moved aside. "I was just leaving—I guess you heard that, didn't you?"

"I wasn't listening!' Finley tapped her knuckles against the pane of glass on the door and waited a moment before opening it. She glanced over her shoulder and saw Brady and Riley making their way toward the bank of elevators.

Doris Farmer, her father's secretary, smiled at her. "Why the knock?"

Finley stepped inside the reception area and closed the door. She sighed heavily, still feeling the aftershock of Brady's presence. "I know there's some touchy meetings going on in here and I didn't want to barge in on something."

Doris nodded. "I understand." She shuffled some papers on her desk and sighed. "This is the time of year I hate most. Want to see the coach?"

"No," Finley said as she sat in one of the green and gold chairs. "I'm supposed to meet Frank here. We've got some pictures to develop."

"How do you like your job so far?" Doris leaned back in her chair and massaged the small of her back.

"So far, so good. Of course, I haven't really done anything yet."

Doris smiled. "Well, get ready! The action starts today. The team's selected, and now things get serious."

The office door opened and Frank strode in. His jaws worked as he chewed a mouthful of potato chips. He swallowed and grinned at Finley.

"Hi! Ready to start work?" He looked at Doris. "Doris, my lovely, we'll be in the photo lab, if anyone cares."

"Okay." Doris winked at Finley. "Try to keep him from washing down those chips with photography chemicals, Finley."

Finley laughed and stood.

"Very funny," Frank said in a growling tone. "Very funny."

Finley waved to Doris, then followed Frank down the hall to the photo lab. Once inside, she lost herself in the chemicals, negatives, and final prints. A few of the shots were good, and she felt her confidence grow when Frank complimented her on the work.

"This stuff is pretty easy, though," he said as he examined the drying prints. "When the season starts, that's when it gets tough. I can't wait!" Frank rubbed his hands together. "The first game is in two weeks! Two weeks." Frank's eyes seemed to glow in the dim light. "Getting excited, Finley?"

"Kind of." Finley poked him in the ribs. "I can see that you're excited."

"Oh, I love it!" Frank switched on the overhead light. "Almost as much as I love food." He rocked his head to one side. "Speaking of food, how about lunch?"

Finley laughed. "You're on." She grabbed her purse. "Frank, do you think I'll be able to handle all this? I've taken football shots before, of course, but—"

"Aw, don't you worry," Frank said with an understanding smile. "You're going to knock 'em dead, Finley."

Finley sighed and glanced once more at the photographs. They're good, she thought, but I can do better. I *must* do better. She followed Frank from the studio and tried to bury the nagging doubts.

Kristi Sinclair's cutting remarks the other evening about how Finley came to be the assistant team photographer wormed their way into her mind. The only way to stop remarks like that was to prove that she could handle the job. No. Not just handle the job. She had to prove that she was a better than average photographer, and she would do just that!

3

Brady's face was a mask of concentration.

Finley watched as a muscle jerked in Brady's jawline. His eyes were slitted against the glare of the sun, but Finley could see the glint of deep blue and the sight reminded her of the sparkle of a sea seen through a grove of trees. She studied his profile, then let her gaze drop to his hands, clenched in tight fists at his side. As she studied his large hands, the fists relaxed and Brady flexed his long fingers.

Again Finley looked at his profile, and her attention was arrested by the web of lines that fanned from the corners of his eyes and beneath them in little half-moons. Now he turned his face from her, and Finley saw that her father had moved to stand beside Brady and was speaking in a low, gruff voice to the quarterback. Brady gave a curt nod and fitted his helmet over his damp, curling hair.

Brady's decisive movement jolted Finley from her minute, dazelike inspection. She shifted her attention to the playing field, then to the scoreboard, and saw that the opposing team was facing a fourth-down, twelve-yard play.

"When you've got your back against a wall, punt!"

Finley grinned as her memory played her father's voice in her mind. How many times has he told me that? she wondered. Seems like that was always his advice whenever I had a problem at school. Punt.

A muffled sound reached her ears, followed by shuffling

activity on the sidelines, and Finley watched the football sail across the blue sky, then dive into a receiver's hands. The football players along the sidelines began to cheer and yell, and Finley swung her camera to catch their enthusiasm. The shutter closed upon Jilly Jackson, who was jumping up and down and screaming, "Go! Go! Go!"

Finley moved aside as the offense flowed onto the field and the defense took their places along the sidelines. Glancing at the scoreboard again, Finley felt her stomach muscles tighten. One touchdown and one field goal behind. Fourth quarter. Finley grimaced. She gazed hopefully at the offensive line and resisted the urge to cross her fingers.

Brady's voice, faint but clear, reached Finley. He called a series of numbers and letters, then the ball was snapped into his hands. Finley held her breath as she watched Brady run backwards. Sunlight glanced off his helmet as he turned his head right and left in search of a receiver. Two hulking streaks of blue and white covered Brady, and Finley sucked in her breath. The crowd roared its approval.

"I wish we were playing at home," Finley muttered.

Lifting her camera, Finley snapped a picture of Brady's sprawled form. The two defenders were standing over him, grinning. Finley snapped another picture, then waited for Brady to find his feet. He stirred, then rose to his hands and knees. The slow, drugged movements triggered an alarm in Finley's brain and her breath came in a painful hiss. Kevin Rogers sprinted to Brady and leaned over to touch the fallen player's shoulder. Brady shook his head and Kevin waved a hand toward the sidelines.

Jeb Allen, the team's doctor, ran toward Brady and Kevin. Finley saw Frank waddle onto the field, his camera clicking wildly. Looking for her father, Finley caught sight of Rick Waverly, the backup quarterback. Rick was tossing a football to another player.

He's warming up his arm, Finley told herself. He thinks Brady's out of the game.

She spied her father and was confused at the lack of interest he was showing. Instead of having a worried look on his face, Mike Malone was listening intently to a bodyless voice that floated to him via his earphones. Doesn't he care that Brady might be—might be hurt? Finley wondered.

Again, she sought out the fallen player, but Brady was on his feet now and the doctor was walking toward the sidelines. As he neared her father, the doctor gave a thumbs-up sign and Finley heard him say, "Just got the breath knocked out of him."

Finley looked at Rick and saw a shadow of disappointment flicker across his face as the sound of halfhearted applause signaled the return of Bryan Brady to the huddle.

Relief feathered through Finley as she watched Brady position himself behind the center. She lifted her camera again and focused it on Brady's green and gold helmet. Shadows hid his features from her as Brady stepped back and handed the ball to a charging teammate. Finley set to work, her finger pressing the shutter button over and over as she followed the scrambling player. Just when it seemed the Wildcatter would gobble no more yardage, he sprinted from beneath flailing arms and legs and Finley sucked in her breath. A whoop escaped her lips as she captured the moment when the Wildcatter crossed the goal line.

"It's Kevin!" she announced to no one in particular. Finley glanced around and watched the gleeful pandemonium. The players were leaping into the air, their fists pounding the air. When Kevin reached the sidelines, he was greeted by slaps on the back and on the rear. Hope surged through Finley as she examined the score. We can win, she thought. We can win!

Instinctively, she sought the man who called the winning signals. Her eyes searched for Number Ten among the celebrating ball handlers. As the defense took the field, Finley spotted Brady. He was sitting on one of the long benches and he held an oxygen mask to his mouth and nose. The doctor was seated next to him and the physician was gingerly touching Brady's ribs.

Was it more than just getting his breath knocked out of him? Finley wondered as she moved closer to Brady and Dr. Allen. The doctor motioned for Coach Malone, and Finley stepped closer to be in earshot.

"I'm taking him in for X rays," Dr. Allen told Coach Malone.

"I'll need him out here," the coach barked.

Dr. Allen shrugged. "If he's okay, I'll send him back in the game. If those ribs are cracked, he could puncture a lung. You want that?"

Mike Malone frowned. "Naw. Just hurry." He touched Brady's shoulder before returning to his post at the sideline.

Puncture a lung! Finley swallowed as a horrible picture formed in her mind. Brady's face suddenly crumpling with pain . . . Finley pulled the curtain down on her imagination and watched the doctor and his assistant help Brady toward the tunnel that led to the dressing rooms.

Moans from the crowd spun her to face the playing field again, and she realized the Wildcatters had intercepted the ball.

"I've got to keep my mind on my job," she told herself. "Can't worry about Brady. Why should I?"

With a determined effort, Finley focused her attention on the game. Number Twelve floated before her viewfinder, and Finley sharpened the camera's focus on Rick Waverly. You've got your chance, Rick, she thought. Let's see what you can do.

Three plays later, Finley positioned herself twenty yards from the line of scrimmage and waited, her camera poised. It would be a pass, and she wanted to capture the moment of reception.

The oblong ball sailed from Rick's hand and Finley tensed, her camera following the brown object. A moan filtered through her lips as she snapped the shutter, capturing an interception. The crowd exploded in ecstasy and Finley heard the groans of the Wildcatters behind her.

Where's Brady? she wondered with irritation. We're going to lose if he doesn't get back out here.

Finley walked toward her father, who was speaking into the headset. As she neared him she heard him speaking urgently in the headset to the spotters who were seated high above the playing field in their glass-walled observation deck. They're searching for a miracle, she thought. Disappointed and tired, Finley glanced across the field at Frank, who was busy snapping pictures.

I should be doing that, she thought. But we're losing! She smiled as she watched Frank run ten yards ahead of the action in a rambling, awkward shuffle.

"I'm back, Coach."

The deep voice was like a shot of adrenaline to her slumped spirits, and Finley turned eagerly toward its owner.

Brady stood beside her father. Finley noticed his pallor and the way his skin seemed to be pinched beneath his eyes and at the corners of his mouth.

"Everything okay?" Coach Malone glanced at Brady.

"Sure. Just bruised."

"Waverly just threw an interception. Hope you can do better than that, Brady."

"I'll try, Coach."

"Better do more than just *try!*" Mike Malone scowled at Brady.

Brady dangled his helmet from the chin strap for a moment, then cleared his throat. "I could get some better passes off if I could get some protection."

"They're giving you plenty of time. Don't bellyache."

"They're not giving me time! Before I can . . ." Brady let the words die as the coach waved an irritated hand.

"Now now, Brady. I ain't your mother." Coach Malone turned his back on Brady, signalling the end of the discussion.

Finley felt her temper flare at her father's dismissal. She looked at Brady, but couldn't catch his eye. Brady was watching the field, his blue eyes moving from side to side. With another scorching glance at her father, Finley stomped along the sidelines and forced herself to concentrate on taking pictures and not on taking sides.

A nagging question wiggled into her mind, and she frowned. Why am I taking sides against my own father? she wondered. Why am I taking Brady's side? She shook her head. It's not my business. My business is taking pictures.

She aimed her camera and started shooting.

Finley buckled her seat belt and stared at the huge flaps on the wings of the airplane. She smiled and felt the familiar tingle of anticipation slice through her as she waited for the engines of the plane to change from a whine to a roar.

Takeoff! Finley wrapped her fingers about the arm rests and planted her feet firmly on the floor. The rumble of masculine voices and the occasional high-pitched giggle of a stewardess reached through Finley's absorption with the wing flaps. She shifted her gaze to the inside of the airplane and wondered who decided that brown and pink were relaxing colors. Makes me feel a bit sick, she thought.

Frank fell into the seat next to Finley and offered her a weak smile. He drew his handkerchief from his pocket and wiped his brow.

"Whew! Almost missed the plane." He replaced the handkerchief and wrestled with his seatbelt. "Bryan and I started playing the pinball machines and forgot the time! We heard the last call for boarding and had to run all the way." Frank rolled his eyes. "Easy for him. Tough for me."

"Are you all right?" Finley touched Frank's arm, noticing how the large man's chest was heaving up and down.

"Yeah. Just out of breath." He leaned back against the headrest. "Whew!"

Finley glanced up in time to see Bryan Brady. A stewardess showed him to a seat—directly across the aisle from Finley. Finley looked across Frank's stomach at Brady.

"Is there anything I can get you, sir?" The stewardess smiled warmly.

"No, thanks."

"Please fasten your seat belt."

"Sure thing." Brady snapped the apparatus, then squirmed deeper into the chair. He turned his head and met Finley's steady stare. His gaze shifted to Frank.

"Hey, ol' buddy. You're huffing and puffing!"

Frank frowned. "I'm not an athlete. Running isn't my favorite thing in the world."

Brady chuckled. "Yeah. Your favorite thing is Snickers and I just happen to have one in my pocket here."

Frank's eyes widened and he looked at Brady. "Where'd you get one?"

Brady pulled the candy bar from his pocket. "Gift shop in the airport." He tossed the candy into Frank's lap. "Bon appetit, compliments of your pinball partner."

"Thanks, Bryan!" Frank shoved the candy bar into his shirt pocket. "This will be the only good thing I'll have to eat on this contraption. Airplane food! Yeeeck!"

Finley shifted in her seat and her gaze caught the sudden movement of Brady's hand when it moved to gingerly touch his rib cage. She furrowed her brow. Must be bruised bad, she thought. She cleared her throat.

"Did they wrap your ribs, Brady?"

Brady seemed surprised at her question, his eyes widening for a moment before he answered. "No. I'm supposed to jump into the whirlpool when I get to Tulsa. I'm just bruised a little."

"Nothing's broken?" Finley asked.

"Naw!" Brady chuckled. "Takes more than a little linebacker to break *my* bones. Did you get some good pictures of me?"

Finley nodded. "I got a real good one when you were

down and those linebackers were standing over you—victorious."

Brady frowned. "Gee, thanks." He turned his head to stare straight ahead.

"I got a picture of you running the ball in for the winning touchdown, too!" Finley added, trying to erase the frown from his face.

Sparkling blue eyes swiveled in her direction. "Did you now?"

Finley felt a smile tug at the corners of her mouth. Brady's lilting question held a definite Irish flavor. "Yes. Don't pout."

He stuck out his bottom lip briefly, then his mouth curved into that dangerous grin. "Have you decided to put down your hatchet? Are we going to be friends?"

Finley felt Frank's gaze switch from Brady to herself, and she tried to ignore his blatant curiosity. "W-e-l-l. I've decided that you might not be such a bad guy if you'd drop that macho, playboy image. Think you could do that when you're around me?"

Brady lowered his head slightly, so that his brows cast a shadow over the glint of his eyes. He looked dangerous. "I am what I am, Finley," he said softly. "I'm not putting on an image and I'm not going to adjust myself to fit *your* image."

Finley felt herself bristle at the soft-voiced put-down. "How disappointing! I assumed that *no one* could be as immature, as conceited, as arrogant as you! I just assumed your playboy routine was an act."

Brady shook his head. "No act." His gaze lifted to follow the lines of a passing flight attendant, and his mouth curved into a sensuous line. "I happen to like women." His blue eyes found hers again. "Even hot-tempered, sharp-tongued, little lassies like you."

Finley narrowed her eyes. "You see women as one-dimensional, don't you? They exist only to pleasure men. I think that's disgusting."

A harsh laugh vibrated his throat. "Grow up, Finley! There's nothing wrong with a man and woman deriving pleasure from one another, and I don't think you should pass judgement until you know what you're talking about."

A flash of temper straightened Finley's spine. "*Now* what are you implying?"

That crooked grin captured his mouth. "Just that you're not exactly a woman of experience." He winked broadly, his gaze meeting Frank's for a split second. "Of course, there's still time."

A sharp retort sprang to her mind, then something else registered. Silence. Finley pulled her gaze from Brady's taunting grin and saw that several of the football players in earshot were openly listening to their machine-gun-fire conversation. Finley felt her cheeks grow hot as she caught Jilly's broad smile. She lifted her chin and glared at Brady.

"Not for you, Brady. My time is too valuable to be wasted on the likes of you."

Brady laughed at her cutting remark. "You know, Finley, you should ease up and enjoy. You might like me, if you'd just relax. I like you." His lazy gaze moved from her flushed face to her throat, the curve of her shoulder, and the outline of her round breasts. "I like your—" The blue eyes found hers again. "I like your mind, Finley."

Several of the football players chuckled knowingly, and Finley saw Kevin elbow Jilly.

Frank cleared his throat and looked uneasy. "Uhhhh." He swallowed. "Finley, would you like to trade seats or—?"

"No." Finley turned her head to stare out the window again. She cautioned herself not to respond to Brady's baiting. He was playing with her for the benefit of the others on the plane, and she refused to be the joke.

"Hey, hey, honey!"

Brady's voice drifted to Finley, but she didn't turn to face him. Was he calling *her* honey?

"Yes, sir?"

The flight attendant's soft purr sent a ripple of disappointment through Finley. She cursed herself for thinking that Brady would waste an endearment on her.

"Could you get me a couple of aspirin?"

"Of course, sir."

"Got a headache, Bryan?" Frank's voice held a note of concern.

"A brain-buster, Frank. Listen, when they serve dinner, you can have mine. Don't let them disturb me, okay? I'm going to get some shut-eye and try to kill this headache."

"Okay, Bryan."

"Here's your aspirin, sir."

"Thanks, doll. Say, do you live in Tulsa by any chance?"

A melodic laugh escaped from the shapely flight attendant, and Finley frowned. She was falling for Brady's smooth-talk. The idiot!

"Why, yes. I live in an apartment there on Riverside Drive."

"No kidding? Well, I jog near there. Maybe I'll see you sometime."

"Maybe." The stewardess's voice lowered to a husky whisper. "I'm in the telephone book—Janet Wilson."

Finley rolled her eyes. How did he do it? She glanced at him from the corner of her eye and saw him recline his seat and rest his head against the cushioned headrest. He closed his eyes and heaved a sigh. Finley noticed the grim set of his mouth, as if he were gritting his teeth. No matter how much pain he was suffering, he always made time to hustle women! She turned back to the window and kept her gaze glued to the dark outside.

She pressed her cheek to the cool glass and felt her anger begin to melt. He really is impossible, she thought. And *I'm* worried about his darn headache and rib cage! She shook her head. She could see how women could get caught up with him, though. He was like a little boy sometimes—almost vulnerable.

She closed her eyes and saw the glint of a cobalt gaze. He's a rascal, she thought. It would be so easy to get tangled up in his life. So easy . . . Especially when he let his guard down and revealed glimpses of a man who wasn't so sure of himself.

Exhaustion weaved through her mind and body, and Finley slept. Vaguely she heard Frank's question of whether or not she wanted her dinner. She shook her head and Frank thanked her, telling her not to worry, he'd eat it up for her.

Finley nodded again and wiggled deeper into sleep. She dreamed that her head rested on Brady's chest instead of the cold, slick window.

It was raining in Tulsa when the airplane finally touched down. Finley sighed and wished for her raincoat as she searched the wet streets for a taxi. A sheet of rain plastered her shirt and jeans to her skin as she raced toward a taxi that was pulling toward the curb.

"Oooops!"

Finley grabbed the taxi's door handle to keep from falling as a body collided with hers. She looked up at the man who had uttered the halfhearted apology. Bryan Brady.

"It's you—of course," Finley said with a frown.

"Sorry, Finley." Brady opened the taxi door. "Want to share or do you want to fight over possession?"

Finley glanced up at the mist of rain and shrugged her shoulders. "We can share."

The inside of the cab was toasty warm, and Finley gave the cab driver her address. Brady gave an address in an old section of the city to the driver.

"You live in that section of town?" Finley asked as the cab drew away from the curb.

"Yes," Brady shook rain drops from his hair. "I bought an

old house near the depot and I'm remodeling it."

"Are you doing the work or have you contracted it?"

"I'm doing most of it," he said, then turned to look at her. "Would you like to see it?"

Finley shook her head. "Not tonight. I'm tired and wet and I wouldn't be good company."

"Sure. I understand." He glanced out the window and said, almost to himself, "Hope the rest of the season goes like it did tonight."

"Have you any doubts?"

Brady looked at her again and smiled. "Lots of them. So much of this stuff is in the hands of fate."

"But we've got a great team! Everybody says so!" Finley sat up straighter.

"Yeah, I know, but that's right now. I'm thinking about possible injuries. Staying healthy is the main thing."

"Oh." Finley glanced down at her wrinkled shirt and noticed that it was drying. "Did you get hurt bad tonight?"

Brady gave her a slow smile. "Hurt? Tonight? No! I just got the breath knocked out of me."

"Yes, but you said you were bruised, too."

Now Brady laughed, a robust sound that swelled in the confines of the taxi. "Show me a player without bruises and I'll show you a player who's benched! *Everybody* gets bruised!"

Finley felt irritation curl in her stomach, but she told herself to stay calm in the face of Brady's hilarity.

He's right, of course, she thought. Bruises and cuts are commonplace among football players. Pulled muscles, leg cramps, and fractures come with the pay checks. Still, why did he always have to laugh? I'm such a big joke to him.

Finley cast a sideways glance at Brady and found that he was watching the passing scenery. A spicy, tangy scent emanated from him and seemed to wrap about her like a warm cloak. She sniffed and tried to decipher the cologne. No. It wasn't familiar to her. He seemed bigger than life to her, seated so close. Her gaze drifted to his muscled thighs, then across his powerful forearms. His neck was wide and strong looking and his shoulders were broad.

A blush touched Finley's cheeks. Dad wouldn't like what you're thinking, Finley, she thought. Better keep your eyes to yourself.

Yet she found her gaze drawn to him again. A streetlight cast a flickering glow across his face for an instant, and Finley noted the slightly crooked nose. Gives him character, she mused. In the dim light of the cab Finley could see the slight protrusion of his lower lip, and she smiled. Looks like he's pouting, she thought. Gives him a little boy charm.

A little boy . . .

Finley caught her breath when a man's frank, appraising stare caught her off guard. Brady's mouth twitched slightly.

"What's the matter?" he asked softly.

"Nothing," Finley lied and looked away from him to the blur outside the cab window.

Fool! she scolded herself. He's not a little boy, and you'd better remember that! She pulled her bottom lip between her teeth to keep it from quivering.

"Something surprised you. What was it?"

Finley edged closer to the door when she felt Brady's breath on her cheek. Now she felt the car seat sink an inch as he laid a hand alongside her leg.

"I was just daydreaming. It's nothing." Finley blinked, then breathed a relieved sigh when she saw her house whip into view. The cab slowed, rolling toward the curb. "Ah! I'm home." She turned to face Brady now and she felt her eyes widen when she found his face not more than an inch from her own. Instinctively, she swayed back until her head touched the cab window. Finley cleared her throat. "H-how much do I owe?"

A knowing smile curved Brady's lips before he leaned closer and allowed his lips to brush hers. "You don't owe me anything, Finley."

Finley slid her hand down the door until her fingers found the door handle. She yanked violently at it and the door popped open. Finley gasped and, for a moment, felt herself falling from the car. Then a strong arm curved about her waist and she was pulled back into the car and crushed to Brady's chest. Finley stared at the buttons on his shirt for a startled moment before she pressed her palms against his chest and tried to put inches between their bodies.

Brady chuckled. "I don't want you falling for me, Finley."

"What?!" Finley tipped her head back to look at the laughter in his blue eyes.

"I said, I didn't want you to fall for me—out of taxis or otherwise. I'd hate to see you get hurt." That lopsided grin captured his mouth.

Finley examined his devilish grin for a few moments and fought the urge to smile back at him. The magnetism of his grin seemed to hold her spellbound. Even as his mouth loomed closer and closer, Finley could not bring herself to turn away from him. She watched and waited.

When his lips touched hers, Finley felt a spark of magic light her soul. As his mouth moved to cover hers, the spark grew until Finley thought it was daybreak instead of midnight. She closed her eyes and felt her mouth curve into a smile when Brady cupped her face between his hands. His mouth left hers, and Finley opened her eyes to find his blue ones.

"Funny, I thought you'd fight me," he whispered.

Finley arched her brows. "Fight you? Over a little kiss? That's rather drastic action isn't it?"

"Is *that* what you call it? Just a *little* kiss?" Brady sounded offended.

Finley smiled a challenge. "What do *you* call it?"

The grin was back again before Brady nodded briefly, accepting her challenge, then bent to his task. The touch of his lips was magic again, or was it sorcery? Finley wondered. His roving mouth cast a definite spell over her and she melted

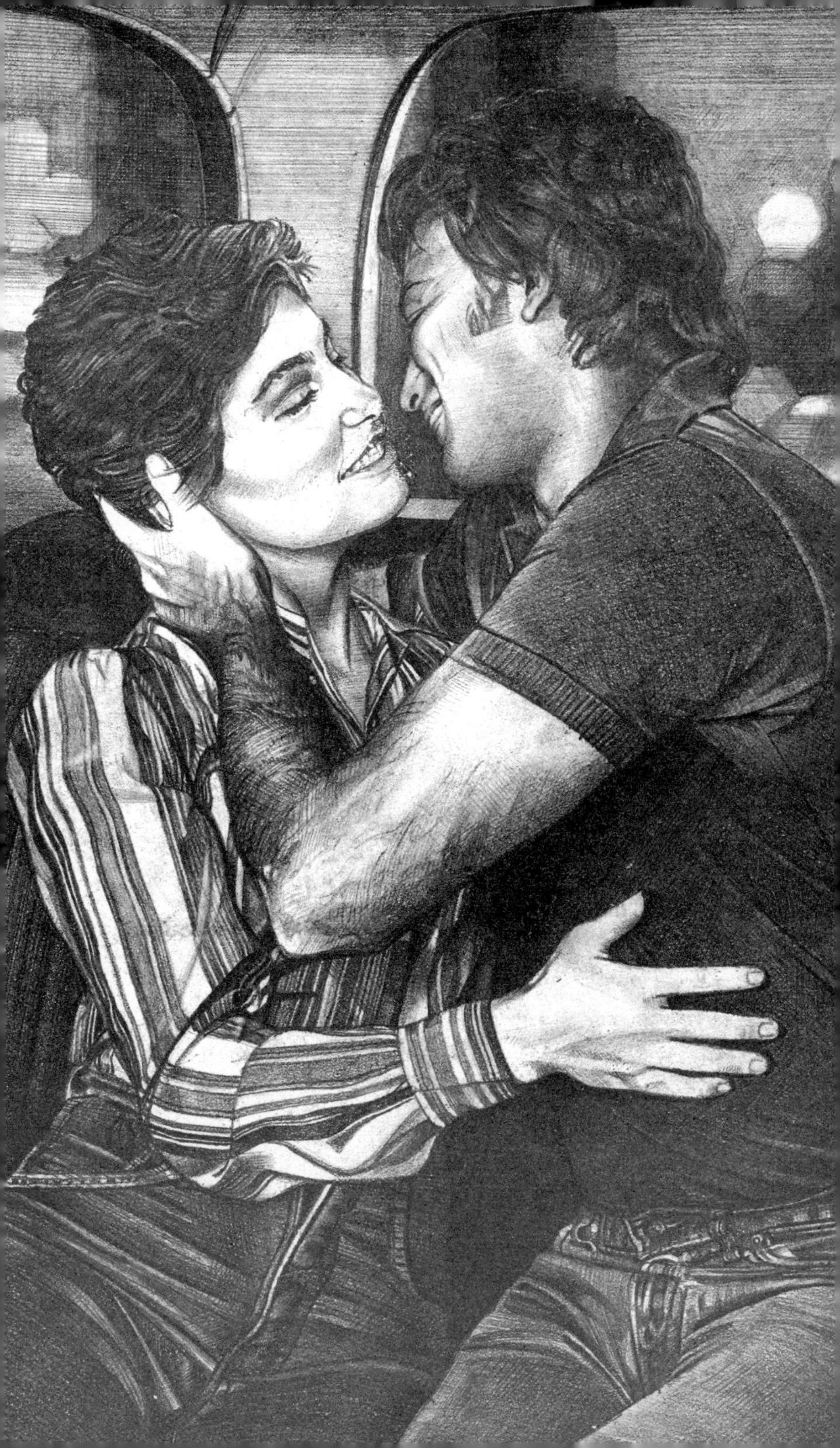

against him as his hands moved from her face to her shoulders, only to slip down her arms to rest on her waist.

He's fast, Finley thought. Before I even have time to acknowledge his movements, he's—

She caught her breath as his tongue darted inside her mouth to tease and tantalize. Her body tensed when his fingers caressed her breasts and whispered across her taut nipples. Finley shivered; the spell was broken. She quickly pushed away from him and scrambled from the taxi.

Swaying slightly, Finley slammed shut the car door and faced Brady's astonished amusement.

"Finley? Are you okay? It was just a little kiss and—"

"Good night, Mister Brady." Finley turned from his dancing eyes.

"Finley! You can't call me mister after *that* kiss! Surely that puts us on a permanent first-name basis."

His voice vibrated with controlled mirth, and Finley balled her hands into fists. She turned to face him again, striving for a normal tone. "Bryan Brady, good night!" She whirled again and walked to the front porch. "Congratulations on the game tonight!"

"Which game?"

Finley squinted her eyes against her anger and unlocked the front door. Don't look back, she thought. If you look back and see him grinning like the Cheshire cat, you'll fly into a tirade. Finley entered her house, closed the door, and suppressed her urge to scream.

4

The emerald green evening gown caught particles of light and seemed to shimmer. Finley turned to the left, then the right, to survey her length in the mirror. Her brow puckered as she ran a critical gaze over her mirrored figure.

"Wish I were taller," she murmured as she lifted one high-heeled sandal. "These shoes just don't lift me enough."

She leaned closer to the mirror to examine her eye makeup. Satisfied, she stepped back and gathered in the reflection once more before she reached for her green and gold shawl. At the soft knock at the door, she called, "Come in, Dad. I'm decent."

Mike Malone stepped inside Finley's bedroom. His eyes widened and he whistled. "You look beautiful! I'm gonna have trouble keeping the guys away from you tonight." He glanced down at the toes of his black shoes and shoved his hands into the pockets of his tuxedo trousers. "You shoulda got you a proper escort, Finley. You didn't have to go with me."

Finley frowned and kissed his tanned cheek. "Dad, you know I love being your special girl. Besides, *you* could have gotten yourself a 'proper' escort, too! I know that Amy Vaughn would be estatic if you'd just ask her out—"

"I'm not interested in her," Mike growled. "I don't have time to mess around with some old widow woman."

"Daddy!" Finley shook her head and straightened her father's bow tie. "What a terrible thing to say! Amy is a wonderful woman and she's quite a looker!"

Mike scowled. "You let *me* decide who I look at and who I don't."

Finley nodded. "Fine. You'll do the same for me?" She laughed. "Come on, Dad. We're going to be late for the big bash if we don't get a move on."

On the way downtown to the large hotel where the annual Wildcatter Ball was held, Finley giggled as her father complained about "these crazy shindigs" and "getting all dressed up for nothing."

"For nothing?" Finley cast him a speculative glance. "Most of the people who attend this thing are season ticket holders who donate lots of money each year to the team."

Mike shrugged as he parked the car in the underground parking lot. "Sure, sure. I know that. But why do we have to get all gussied up? Let *them* have their dance and let *me* stay home and watch television."

Finley laughed and waited for him to round the car and open her door. She climbed out of the car and kissed his cheek. "I'm glad you're all dressed up. You look adorable. Now, come on and escort your daughter to this silly old dance."

Mike grinned and led her toward the double doors that marked the entrance to the hotel. Once inside, they took an elevator to the forty-ninth floor, and when the doors slid open, Finley could hear the strains of a sweeping love tune. A formally attired man stood outside the golden doors; he bent at the waist when he spied Finley and Mike.

"Good evening, Coach Malone, Miss Malone." He opened the doors and nodded.

Finley felt a tingle race up her spine as she entered the huge hall and the color, movement, and sounds caught her in a whirlwind. She stood just inside the doorway and watched the blur of expensive evening gowns and dashing tuxedos before Mike's hand at her waist urged her forward to the head table. Her father was greeted on every side as they made their way to the table. Finley smiled at the owner of the team and the assistant coaches who were already seated at the table. She greeted their wives and daughters before sitting near the center of the table, where a waiter poured golden champagne into a glass before her.

A mixture of excitement and dread ribboned through Finley as she sipped the tangy liquid. She acknowledged the comments that floated around her, but found it difficult to concentrate on the table talk. Instead, Finley examined the people in the room. Dressed formally, they looked like royalty instead of like the football players she knew. She found herself fascinated with the players' dates. Many of the players were accompanied by their wives, but the single men had dates, and Finley didn't see a homely face among them.

They all look like models, she told herself. Not a flaw anywhere. She shrugged and hummed: *You gotta be a football hero to get along with the beautiful girls.*

Kristi Sinclair swept into Finley's line of vision, and right behind her was Bryan Brady. Finley tensed, then forced herself to relax. Heavens! Every time you see that man you get all bent out of shape! Finley tipped her head to one side and examined Kristi. What would it be like to be a professional cheerleader? she wondered. I've heard the pay scale isn't anything to brag about. Kristi *must* have another job. Finley noted the black, form-fitting evening gown Kristi wore and the high, high heels. The outfit was striking coupled with Kristi's blond hair and pale complexion.

Shifting her attention to Brady, Finley found herself staring into his dark blue eyes. He smiled and nodded slightly, and Finley felt her color rise in a tide of embarrassment. It's as if he can read my thoughts, she mused. Of course, that's stupid! Finley squared her shoulders and turned to converse with a dinner companion. She forced herself to show an interest and vowed not to look in Brady's direction again throughout the rest of the evening.

Concentrating on the carefully prepared dinner, Finley found herself attacking the meal as if it were her last supper. Chiding herself, she forced a slower pace during dessert and tried to shake the feeling of being stared at by a pair of midnight blue eyes.

He's *not* looking at you! she told herself. He's talking to Kristi and the people at his table. He's *not* staring at you.

Finally, just to convince herself, Finley decided to allow herself a quick peek. She cautiously turned in her seat and looked up to confront a frilled shirtfront and a black, satin vest standing before her.

Bryan Brady smiled at her as his eyebrows rose in surprise.

Finley swallowed, then searched for her voice. "What are you doing standing there?"

His smile twitched with amusement. "I've come to ask you to dance. Will you?"

"Dance?" Finley leaned to one side to peer around him and saw the couples gliding to the tune of a love song. "Oh. Dance!"

"Yes. You know, Finley, you are quite remarkable. I don't think I've ever seen a person concentrate so totally on a dinner plate and its contents in my life. Fascinating."

"So!" Finley placed her hands on the edge of the table for support. "You *were* staring at me all evening!"

He shook his head. "Not *all* evening. Shall we dance?"

"No." Finley glanced down at her hands and saw that her knuckles were white. She relaxed her grip.

"Now, now." Brady almost crooned the words. "Don't be such a child, Finley. Dance with me."

Finley shook her head. "Get lost, Brady. I want to enjoy this evening."

"Listen, Red."

Finley's gaze flew to his face at the nickname. Red? He's calling me Red?

". . . and we want to get him something real nice. I wanted to talk to you about it. Now, dance with me!"

Startled and confused, Finley gasped when Brady wrapped the fingers of one hand about her upper arm and hauled her to her feet. She swayed slightly, then found herself being shoved toward the crowded dance floor. His arm wrapped about her waist and she felt herself being pulled forward until not a breath of space existed between their bodies.

"Brady," she said his name between clenched teeth. "Back off a little before I make a scene."

His blue eyes searched her face for a moment, then his grip lessened. "You know, we could have fun if you'd stop fighting me."

"I might stop fighting you if you'd stop pushing me around and acting as if I were a rag doll."

His eyes smiled. "Okay, okay. Let's talk about that gift."

"What gift?"

Brady frowned. "That gift I was talking about just a few seconds ago."

"Brady, this might come as a complete surprise to you, but I don't hang on your every word. I wasn't listening to you."

His chest lifted in a sigh. "I was talking about the fact that the guys and I want to get your dad something real special for his birthday and I was wondering if you'd go shopping with me next week to try and find something."

Finley moaned. "Oh, Brady, not next week!"

"It's got to be next week. We're going to be out of town for the following two weeks, and then it's his birthday."

"What?" Finley counted the days quickly. "You're right! I haven't picked him up anything either."

"So, we'll go shopping next week."

Finley moaned again. "But, I'm moving next week and I've got a million things to do."

"Moving? Where are you moving to?"

Finley chewed on her bottom lip for a few moments, her mind whirling. "I— I'm moving to an apartment near the university."

"Oh yeah?" Brady grinned. "Moving away from home, huh?"

"I've lived by myself for four years, Brady," Finley told him in a dry tone. "I was just staying with Dad until I could find an apartment close to the practice field."

"Tell you what, Red. I'll help you move if you'll help me find a gift for your dad. Okay?"

Finley eyed him for a few moments, suspicious of his offer. "I really don't need the help, Brady. Jilly and Gena offered to help me."

"Well, with one more strong back helping you move, you'll get done a lot quicker and then we can go out and shop for your dad. Okay?"

Finley shrugged. "Okay. I'm moving Wednesday."

"Great. I'll be at your dad's place Wednesday morning. How's that? Good? Great. Then Thursday, we'll shop. I want to get something really special this year because the guys and I think it's going to be a winning year for the team. Got any ideas?"

"Not offhand. I'll give it some thought."

The music ended and Finley gently wormed out of Brady's embrace. She stood before him for several seconds and found herself content just to watch the play of emotions on his face.

"Why did you call me Red?" The question escaped her without any intention, and Finley took a step back in surprise.

Brady grinned. "Fits you, I guess."

Finley swallowed. "Why—why don't you just call me by my name?"

Brady shrugged. "I like nicknames. Why don't you call me by my first name?"

"I—I don't know. I guess I like your last name. *It* fits *you*."

His smile widened to accompany a low, resonant laugh. "One more dance, Finley? Please?" He caught her hands in his.

"I don't know, Brady. Don't you think you're being rude? Kristi's your date."

Slowly, he pulled her to him. "Kristi doesn't own me," he whispered as his arms stole around her waist.

Finley smiled and locked her fingers behind his neck, her palms pressing against the firm muscles there. Devilment danced within her as the beat of a samba pulsated in the room. It was a slow, seductive tune that seemed to weave a sensuous spell within her. Finley marvelled at how light Brady was on his feet. With skillful, quick steps, he guided her about the area, and Finley could feel eyes upon them. She looked up at him, wondering if he, too, could feel the stares.

She found herself caught in the depths of blue velvet eyes and she found it impossible to look away. She was intrigued with the patterns in his irises. Light blue, jagged lines webbed the darker blue background, and his pupils were only a shade darker than that blue. The blue depths seemed warm and secure, yet dangerous and chilling all at the same time.

"You know, Red, you're a dangerous woman."

She didn't comment, other than lifting her eyebrows in question. Her heart had found a nesting place in her throat and was beating there.

"You're the type of woman that grows on a man." He bent his head and his lips caressed the skin of her shoulder. "The more I'm with you, the more I want you."

Finley trembled, and her fingers slid up his neck to brush through the curls on the back of his head. His hands rested in the curve of her back, pressing her closer until she was no longer a stranger to the taut muscles of his thighs. Her breasts were crushed to the wall of his chest, and Finley tipped her head back to smile into his eyes—eyes that were shadowed now with the stirrings of passion. His lips were soft against her temple where a pulse quickened to life and his hands moved up and down her spine as his mouth finally settled over hers. He shifted his lips to better cover her own,

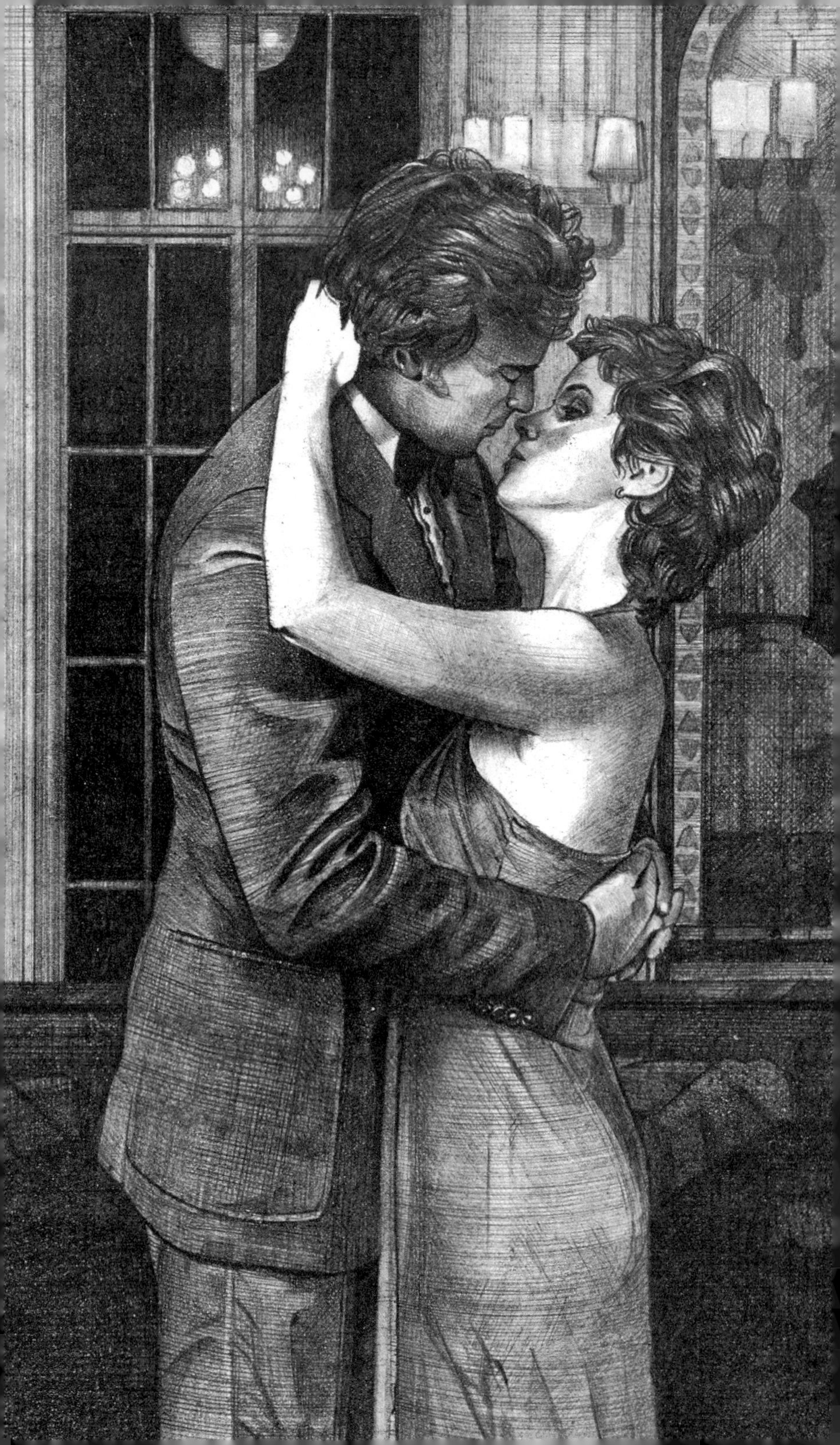

surrounding them in a warm embrace, before she parted her lips to allow the tip of his tongue entrance.

All thoughts of where she was fled her mind as Brady deepened his kiss until his tongue danced with her own. A heady passion burst within her, and Finley's fingers wrapped themselves more firmly in his hair and pulled him closer still until she could feel every muscle and every nuance of his body. He lifted his mouth from hers and his chest expanded as he sucked in air. Finley opened her eyes to stare into the naked longing harbored in Brady's glittering gaze. The music had ceased, but a wild beat pounded within Finley, a tempo ancient and understood only by lovers.

"Pardon me. May I cut in?"

Irritation washed over Finley as Brady's arms left her and he stepped aside with reluctance to examine the intruder.

"Why, sure, Coach. Sorry if I've been monopolizing your daughter." Brady ran a finger around his shirt collar and winked at Finley. "It's kind of warm in here, isn't it?" He smiled quickly, then walked from the dance floor and toward his table.

"Don't look so disappointed, Finley." Mike smiled at her. "I promise I won't step on your toes, though I must admit I can't hold a candle to Bryan's fancy dancing."

Finley smiled and took up the beat of the music. Her father's steps were slower and more routine. "I'm not disappointed Dad."

"Can't fool me, Finley. Everyone's been watching you two out here and I decided to cut in before you made a bigger spectacle of yourself or before Kristi challenged you to a hair-pull."

Finley blushed and wondered what had gotten into her. She'd *never* behaved in such a wanton manner before!

"You falling for his Irish charms, my girl?"

"Irish charms?" Finley sucked in her breath. "No. We—the music—" Finley shook her head. "I'm sorry, Dad. I don't know what I was thinking to—"

"Sure, sure." Her father's voice was light and dismissing. "Just thought you ought to grab a hold of yourself before it's too late."

"Dad, don't be silly." Finley tried to ignore the gnawing panic in the pit of her stomach.

"I'm not being silly. People are starting to talk about you and Bryan, and that—that display just now didn't help the situation."

"I can't help it if people jump to ridiculous conclusions. He just—just kissed me."

"Ha!" Her father gave her a stern look. "Is *that* what you young folks call just a kiss? In my day—"

"Dad, let's drop it!" Finley clamped her teeth together.

"Don't snap my head off." Her father frowned. "I'm just running interference for you."

How about not interfering? The question teetered on the tip of Finley's tongue, but she swallowed the urge to voice it and forced a tense smile to her lips.

The song ended and Finley walked stiffly back to her chair. She refused to meet the curious stares of her table companions, and she found herself wishing the evening was over. She sighed and remembered how much she had been looking forward to the evening. That had been before Brady's lips had awakened a hot, searing passion within her. Even now, she felt shaky and her skin still tingled from his touch. She felt the glittering gaze again, and she lifted her eyes to meet it. Brady smiled at her and she returned the smile.

Heaven help me, Brady, she thought as her smile grew to match his. I like you. Despite all my good intentions and all my inbred common sense, I like you.

When he winked, she winked back and didn't care if anyone else saw it.

5

The red wine gurgled into the waiting glasses, and Finley raised her goblet in a toast.

"To good friends and strong backs!"

Gena, Jilly, and Brady laughed and touched their glasses to hers. Finley felt the wine heat her stomach and spread warmth throughout her body. She sighed and relaxed on the couch, her gaze traveling about the crowded living room. Boxes littered the area and furniture was placed helter-skelter.

"It will take me weeks to sort all of this out," she said with a sigh.

"You're right there, especially since you won't be in town very much for the next few weeks," Jilly observed.

"Oh, that's right." Finley rested her head in one hand. "The next two games are out of town, aren't they?"

"Yes. We won't be in Tulsa until next month." Brady settled onto the couch. "October fourteenth, to be exact. You'll be living out of boxes for a while."

"Who wants this last piece of pizza?" Jilly looked at each person, then grinned. "*I* won't turn it down."

"I've never seen you turn down food, come to think of it," Gena teased.

"I'm a growing boy, Gena." Jilly took a large bite of the pizza, then licked his lips.

"Well, when you've finished that off, we'd better go. I'm

beat and there's a television special on tonight I want to see."

Finley straightened. "Thanks for helping me, you guys. It would have been impossible without you. I'll invite you over for dinner when I get my pots and pans out of those boxes."

Gena waved a dismissing hand. "Don't worry about it. It was fun. Ready, Jilly?"

"Yes." Jilly stood and stretched, his fingertips brushing the ceiling. "You can watch television, but *I'm* going to bed. Good night, Finley. See you tomorrow, Bryan."

"Good night." Finley followed them to the front door and laughed when Brady had to push boxes aside so the door could be opened. She waved a final good night to Jilly and Gena, then turned to find Brady stretched out on the couch.

"You look comfortable." She walked toward the couch, stopping just in front of it.

"You look desirable." Brady's hand slid up Finley's leg, halting at the back of her knee. "Care to join me?"

"Where?" Finley raised a questioning eyebrow, trying to look casual even though the caress of his fingers on the soft skin behind her knee was sending tiny tremors through her until she felt weak.

"Here." Brady grinned and patted the inch of space at his side.

Finley shook her head. "I don't think I'd fit."

"Sure you would." Brady's hand curved around her knee and he pulled.

Finley gasped, feeling her knees buckle, and she flung out her hands to break her fall. Her palms made contact with Brady's chest and she found herself staring into his laugh-filled eyes. Her legs dangled off the side of the couch, and Brady reached down to pull her legs up to rest against his own.

"Brady! What do you think you—?"

Brady's mouth covered hers, successfully halting the remainder of her exclamation. The feel of his fingers tracing her backbone sent shivers through her, and she matched him kiss for kiss. A sweet awareness flowed through her as she squirmed for a more comfortable position atop his powerful frame. He murmured her name, and his hands pressed her closer.

"Alone, at last." His voice held a note of humor. "I've wanted to finish what we started on that dance floor; haven't you, Finley?"

She kissed his shoulder, then lifted her head to drown in his eyes. "Yes." The memory of his kiss and the grim warning of her father sent conflicting feelings warring inside her. "Brady—?"

"Hmmmm?" His mouth was nibbling gently at the base of her throat.

"Dad says people are talking about us."

"Let them talk." His hands slid up in a smooth caress until his fingers buried themselves in her hair.

"If you didn't have such a—a scandalous image." Finley frowned, then smiled as his fingers tightened about the curls of her hair to bring her mouth to his. She traced the outline of his mouth with the tip of her tongue and a burst of power coursed through her when he moaned and captured her lips in an embrace of fiery passion. When his lips released hers, his breath was ragged and his eyes were glazed with unspent passion. Slowly, his expression changed to curiosity and his hands left her hair to feather along her back.

"And what's my 'image'?" His voice was low and husky.

"Oh, that you're a womanizer."

He gave a curt nod. "I have no quarrel with that. Never met a woman I couldn't get along with."

His hands slipped beneath the hem of her shirt to glide effortlessly along her heated skin. Finley threw back her head and closed her eyes as his mouth moved to the opening of her blouse.

"Finley." His lips moved against her skin in a caress and his fingers teased her breasts. "Let's get off this couch and find someplace comfortable."

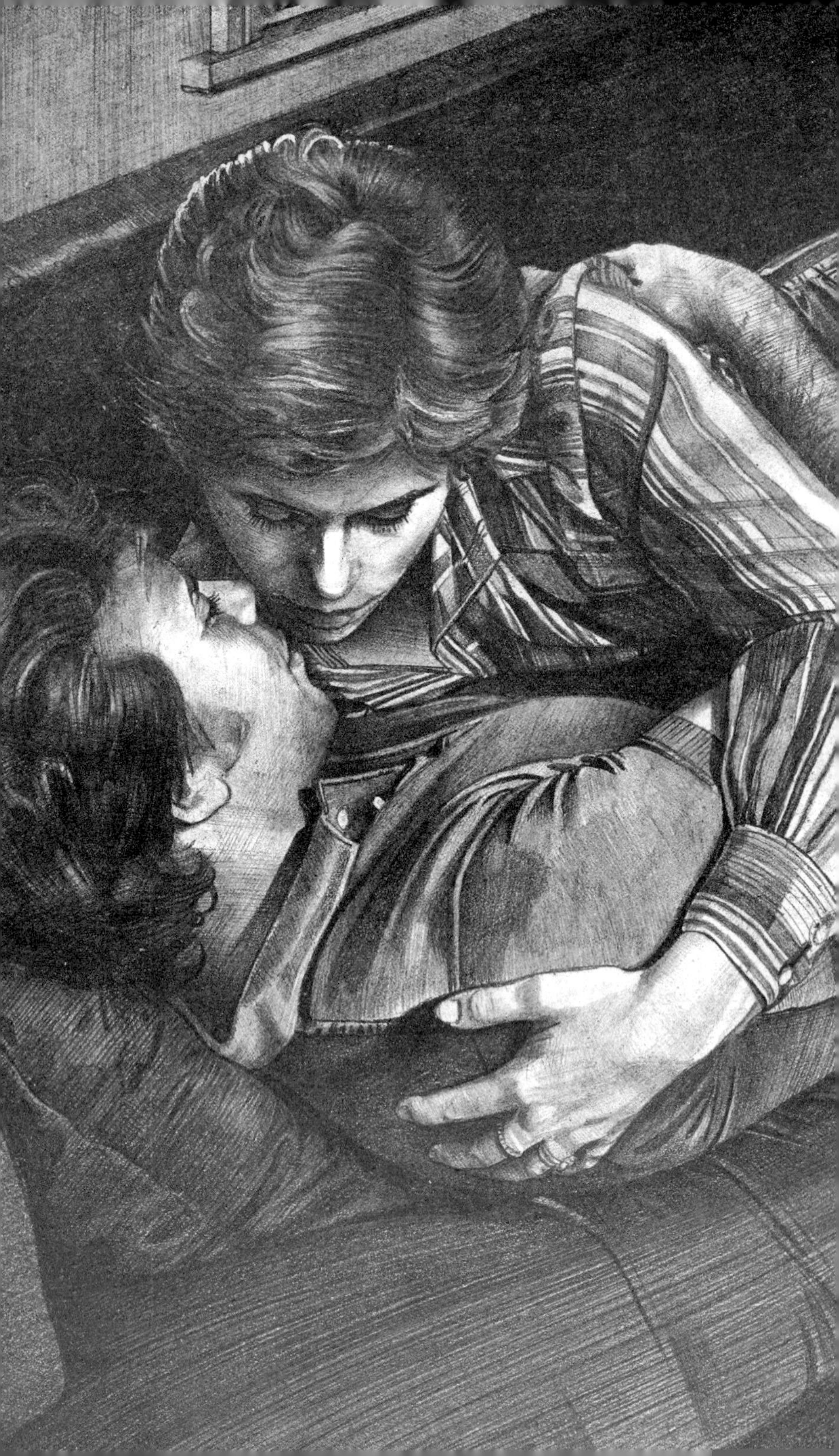

Caution clawed at her senses and she opened her eyes to stare at the curling, burnished hair that covered his scalp. He lifted his head to meet her wavering resolve.

"Finley, come on. You want me as much as I want you. Quit fighting nature."

"Nature?" The word tasted bitter on her tongue. "Is that all this is? Nature? The call of the wild?"

He scowled and tightened his hands at her waist. "Don't start an argument. Not now!"

"I'm—I'm—" Finley shook her head, trying to sort out her jumbled thoughts. "Don't you feel anything special for me?"

A glint of caution flickered deep in his eyes. "Well, yes—in a way . . ."

She hated his hesitancy. He was trying to cover all the bases, she thought. She wasn't special—just available.

"Great." Finley moved quickly before he could react. She bounded from the couch and stood over him, looking down at his shocked expression. "I think you'd better go, Brady. Your fast-talking has given me a headache."

His expression hardened and he stood slowly to his feet to tower over her. "You're a tease, Finley."

"I'm not!" Finley balled her hands at her side. "I'm just immune to your sweet-talking."

"I was trying to be honest! For heaven's sake, Finley, we've just met! You *are* special, but—"

"You're right." Finley spun to stride with purpose toward the door. "We've barely met and now's the time to say good night. Good night."

He plucked his jacket from a chair and walked toward her with angry steps. "I'm getting the bum's rush, right?" He paused in the doorway. "I'll pick you up to go shopping tomorrow around noon."

"Fine." Finley couldn't meet the anger in his eyes.

"Finley." His fingers curled under her chin to lift it, making her stare into his fury-filled eyes. "Next time you find yourself in a—compromising position with me, think twice about changing your mind. I'm not one of your college boyfriends. The only games I play are on the football field." He let his hand drop to her shoulder, then he turned and left.

Finley slammed shut the door, then leaned against it. Why do I *always* fall to pieces around him? she wondered. With any other man, I'm a mature woman. With Bryan Brady? I'm sixteen years old again and trying to act all grown up and doing a terrible job.

She turned off the light and edged around the boxes that littered the floor. Her bed seemed to be calling her, and she opted for a bath in the morning.

She'd have to see him again tomorrow, she thought with grim resolve. Dressing for bed, she repeated the scene in her head, recalling with delicious tremors the way his hands had gentled her and the way his lips had pleasured her. Wearily, she collapsed on the bed. A frown puckered her brow.

So, he didn't think she was anything special—only in a way. What of it? Did she expect him to tell her that she was his one and only? A self-derisive laugh tumbled from her. Not when he could have his pick of beautiful, intelligent women! Finley snuggled deeper into the mattress and closed her eyes. If he didn't take her seriously, then she'd have to keep a safe, friendly distance from him. Another scene like tonight would prove fatal to her heart. He was right. He wasn't anything like the men she'd dated in college. He could arouse in her hot emotions she'd never felt before, emotions that clouded her good sense and flooded her with an overwhelming need to know him and have him know her in the most intimate ways.

When had the tables turned? When had she stopped fighting him and started longing for him? A lazy smile curved her mouth. On that dance floor, she mused. On that dance floor when he had looked at her and she had seen all the promises of fullfillment in his eyes.

Sleep blurred her thoughts, and she slept, to dream of a perfect number ten.

• • •

"I just don't know, Brady!"

Finley shifted her shopping bag from one arm to the other and sighed as she picked her brain for an idea for a present for her father.

"Think!" Brady sounded irritated and tired of the shopping expedition. "I helped you select those cuff links and that tie tack for him; now you've got to help me think of something really special for the team to get him." Brady snatched the shopping bag from Finley and shook his head at her feeble protest. "I'll carry it."

"Let's grab some lunch and discuss it over a good meal and a tall glass of something wet. How does that sound?"

Brady didn't look too thrilled, but he shrugged and nodded.

"You don't want to eat lunch?"

"I'm short on time, Finley. We've got to hurry."

"We've got all day," Finley protested.

He shook his head and sunlight glanced off his red/gold hair. "*You've* got all day. I've got to work out this afternoon."

"Work out?"

Brady stopped and pointed to a small restaurant. "How's this?"

"Look, if you'd rather not take the time—"

Brady ushered her inside the restaurant and motioned her toward one of the booths. A waitress set two glasses of water on the table and gave them menus. Finley glanced over the top of the menu at Brady. His cobalt blue eyes scanned the menu and a frown dipped the corners of his mouth. He'd been in a foul mood all day, and Finley knew it was the residue of last night when he'd left her in a fit of rejected rage. She'd attempted a light, friendly banter, but he'd shunned her weak attempts at cajoling him.

"I mean it, Brady." Finley lowered the menu. "If you'd rather not take the time for lunch, I understand."

"It's okay." He sounded brusque. "You just do some fast

thinking while you eat." He turned to the waitress. "Two cheeseburgers, fries, a salad with French dressing, and a large Coke." He looked at Finley. "What about you, Red?"

Finley shook her head and grinned at the waitress's shocked expression. "I can't top that. I'll have a tuna salad sandwich and a glass of iced tea, please."

"I thought you said you were hungry."

Finley wrinkled her nose. "I am, but I'm not *starved*. Did you say you have to work out this afternoon?"

"That's right."

"Why do you have to?"

He looked at her in obvious surprise. "Why? Well, to stay in shape, of course."

"I should think the regular practices and the games would do the trick."

He shrugged and drank his water. "I'm paranoid, I guess. I never take chances, because I'm afraid I'll get cut from the team if I let down."

"Cut from the team? You?" Finley laughed. "Fat chance they'd cut their quarterback from the team."

Brady fingered the empty water glass for a few moments, his fingertips wiping away the condensation. "You never know, Finley. When you start thinking you're great and that you've got it made, you usually lose everything."

"You *are* paranoid!" Finley tipped her head to one side, trying to fathom this new side of Bryan Brady.

A small smile played at one corner of his mouth. "I'm realistic." He looked up from the empty glass. "So. Let's talk about Mike's gift. Got any ideas?"

"Let me see." Finley rested her chin in her hand. "Maybe something he can display in his office."

"Hmmmm." Brady mirrored her position. "Yeah, that sounds good." Suddenly, he straightened. "I've got it!"

"What?"

"I was in an art gallery the other day and I saw a terrific painting of this wildcat! It was great! It was done in blacks and tans and yellows. Really striking. Do you think he'd like something like that?"

"Sure! That sounds great. It would look nice in his office—right behind his desk." Finley paused a moment and studied Brady while the waitress placed the various dishes and plates before them. "What were you doing in an art gallery?"

"Just looking around." Suddenly his eyes met hers, and a hard glint appeared. "And I don't like the insinuation in your voice, either."

Finley swallowed and lowered her lashes. "I—I just didn't figure you for an art lover, that's all."

"Yes, well, we've already gone over your low opinion of me, so let's just drop the subject." His voice was diamond hard. "We'll go to the gallery when we're finished here. It's just a couple of blocks down the street."

"Fine." Finley bit her lower lip and wished she had curbed her tongue sooner. To insinuate that he wasn't the type to appreciate or understand art was simply bad manners. She glanced at him through the shadow of her lashes. "Brady, I *am* sorry. Are—are you an art collector?"

"I'm looking for a few things for my home." He fixed his attention on the meal, silently ordering Finley to do the same.

Barely tasting the tuna sandwich, Finley mulled over her ability to get tangled up where Bryan Brady was concerned. She watched him attack the two burgers, fries, and salad and marvelled that he could keep his weight down. Frank should be so lucky, she thought with a smile.

"What's so funny?"

Finley jumped as if she'd been caught stealing. "I—I was just thinking that Frank would love to eat as much as you and never gain a pound."

"Well, Frank wouldn't gain a pound if he exercised as much as I do."

"That's true." Finley let her gaze rest on the width of his shoulders, the strong column of his neck, the expanse of his chest that seemed to strain against the material of his gold sweater. With a sigh, she pushed aside her plate.

"That's *all* you're going to eat?" Brady gave her a chiding look.

"I lost my appetite." Finley glanced at her half-eaten sandwich.

"Maybe you're in love."

Finley sucked in her breath and her gaze flew to collide with his mocking eyes. She narrowed her eyes. "I suppose you're used to women falling in love with you."

"You never get used to a thing like that, Red. Are you ready to go?"

She gave him a curt nod and left the booth. Matching his quick strides, Finley followed Brady to the gallery. Inside, a woman in her forties greeted Brady.

"Bryan! How good to see you!" She tucked her slim hand in the crook of his arm and turned her soft, brown eyes up to his face. "Interested in buying something this time?"

Brady kissed her cheek. "As a matter of fact, I am, Alicia. Oh, let me introduce you to a friend of mine. Alicia Spencer, this is Finley Malone."

"Hello, Finley. Any friend of Bryan's is a friend of mine."

"Thank you." Finley examined the woman's dark brown hair that was laced with white and styled in a short, becoming bubble cut. Deep dimples appeared at either side of her wide mouth when she smiled, and Finley liked the kindness she saw in the woman's sable eyes. "Are you the owner of the gallery?"

"Yes. I wanted to show my own art work, so I opened a gallery. Pretty desperate, wouldn't you agree?"

Finley laughed. "Pretty enterprising."

"Well, what are you interested in, Bryan?"

Brady pointed to the painting. "That. How much?"

Finley looked at the painting and smiled. It was perfect. Her father would love it. The wildcat was created with flowing, sweeping lines of browns, golds, and white and its eyes were an alluring golden green. It crouched in a tree and looked quite menacing.

"That?" Alicia's thin brows arched. "Well, I hadn't thought of selling it. I painted it, you know."

"You?" Brady's eyes widened in surprise. "Great! I want to buy it for Coach Malone. His birthday is in two weeks."

"For the coach?" Alicia smiled and placed her hands on her slim hips. "I'll part with it, then. I'm an admirer of Coach Malone. I'll make you a good deal."

"An admirer?" Brady smiled at Finley. "This is the coach's daughter, Alicia."

Alicia turned wide, brown eyes on Finley and a soft pink color flushed her cheeks. "Oh! I—I didn't catch your last name in the introduction. I hope I wasn't out of line to say that I admired your father."

Finley laughed. "Not at all. As a matter of fact, I admire him, too."

Alicia looked relieved, then she laughed a throaty, lusty laugh. "I guess I have a soft spot for Irishmen. That's why I put up with the likes of you, Bryan."

Brady laughed, then pulled his eyebrows together in a thoughtful scowl. "Listen, why don't you come to the presentation? Don't you think it would be appropriate for the artist to be on hand when we give your dad his gift, Finley?"

"Yes." Finley turned to Alicia, placing a hand over her arm. "Will you come?"

Alicia started to shake her head, then seemed to change her mind. "I'd love it!"

Brady paid Alicia for the painting while Finley browsed among the art and sculpture. She was examining a painting of the Tulsa skyline when Brady found her again.

"There you are. Let's go. I'm—"

Finley sighed. "I know. You're late and you've got to work out."

"That's right."

Finley glanced at her watch as they hurried toward

Brady's sports car. "Do you have a date tonight?" She tried to keep her tone casual.

He settled himself behind the wheel, then threw her a wary glance. "Why? Are you asking me out?"

"No." Finley willed her temper to cool. "I just thought that you were probably in a hurry to meet—uh . . ."

"I told you I have to work out. They close the gym at seven." He backed the car from the parking space and sped toward the main street. "Do you want to go out to dinner with me tonight?"

The question threw her off guard, but she stopped the ready agreement that sprang to her lips. An evening with Brady would be courting disaster and a replay of the situation she was trying to avoid. "No. I've got plans."

"Oh?"

She hated the doubt in his voice. "Has it ever occurred to you that I might be involved with someone?"

He cocked an eyebrow. "I don't see a wedding ring on your finger, so I figure you're fair game."

Finley narrowed her eyes and venom seeped through her. "From what I hear, marriage doesn't stop you from hunting."

He narrowed his eyes until they were blue slits and jammed the brakes harder than necessary at a red light. "What does that mean?"

The chipped ice voice sent shivers through her and she felt herself back down. "Nothing. Forget it."

"Yes. Just forget it." The light changed and he gunned the car through the intersection.

Finley clasped and unclasped her hands in her lap. She'd caught a glimpse of his Irish temper then and she was surprised she'd turned tail and run. That wasn't like her. Of course, she'd never really butted heads with an Irishman. She'd learned long ago not to argue with her father. He always won. Finley glanced sideways at Brady's rock-hard jawline and heavy-lidded eyes. Just like Dad, she thought. Impossible!

Finley stood outside her father's office and tapped her foot impatiently. She looked down the hall again, and still there was no sign of Brady.

Where *is* he? Finley recalled the drawn, tired expression he'd worn last night on the flight home. Two weeks on the road had sapped him of strength, and she knew he was uncomfortable. The doctor had said Brady had a bruised thumb socket and Brady had insisted it only ached a little. But Finley could tell that his thumb was swollen after the game. No wonder, she mused. Nothing like having a ball slammed against a bad bruise over and over again!

Footsteps sounded, and Finley glanced up to see Brady. He shook his head and frowned.

"Sorry I'm late, Red. I had to soak my thumb and then the doctor gave me a little lecture on taking care of myself." He glanced about. "Where's Alicia?"

Finley tilted her head. "In Dad's office. She's hanging the painting. Where are the other guys? Dad will be here any minute."

"They're still stuck in practice, but they said to go ahead with the presentation. Let's go into the office and surprise him there." Brady pushed open the door and grinned at Doris. "Hi, beautiful."

"Hello, Bryan! I hear you banged up your hand pretty bad—your throwing hand."

"It's nothing." Brady wagged the injured thumb at her. "I just bruised it. Some big oaf stepped on my thumb."

"The doctor said he almost fractured his hand," Finley told Doris.

"It's just bruised. 'Almost' doesn't count." Brady scowled at Finley. "Come on, Dr. Malone."

Finley resisted the urge to stick out her tongue and followed him into her dad's office. Alicia stood near Mike's desk, her back to them. Finley gasped with pleasure when she saw the painting. It drew the eye like a magnet and added a whole new feeling to the office.

"That looks fantastic, Alicia." Brady placed his hands on Alicia's narrow shoulders. "You're quite an artist."

"It's beautiful. He's going to love it." Finley smiled at Alicia, then whirled when she heard Doris greet Mike. "Hi, Dad!"

"Well, hello. What are you doing here? Hey, Bryan!" Mike paused, confusion marking his brow as he looked at Alicia. Then his gaze was pulled to the painting and his bright, green eyes widened. "What the—? What's this?"

"Happy Birthday!"

The chorus of voices sent a red wave of color over Mike's face and he glanced down at his shoes, then up at the painting again.

"Happy Birthday? I—I—don't know what to say. The picture is just—just—great!" Again Mike looked at Alicia, and confusion marked his face.

"Dad, this is the artist. Alicia, this is Coach Mike Malone," Finley offered.

"No introduction needed on my part," Alicia said and extended her hand. "I'm an admirer of you from way back, Coach. Do you remember me?"

"Alicia—Crockett!" Mike grinned. "Of course I remember you! You were a cheerleader at Notre Dame!"

"And you were the star running back," Alicia finished the thought. "I didn't think you'd remember."

A cheerleader? Finley stared at Alicia, then her father, then Brady. Brady looked shocked, too.

"Well, I'll be! Alicia, how have you been? Do you live here?"

"Sure do. I moved here fourteen years ago with my husband," Alicia said, then added quickly. "I'm a widow. Carl died three years ago."

"Ah! I'm a widower myself. I lost my Emily a long time ago." Mike looked at the painting again. "You're talented, Alicia. Very talented. I sure like it."

"Do you? Oh, I'm so pleased."

"Well, listen, Coach," Brady said, then cleared his throat and waited for Mike to turn to him. "Happy Birthday and all that. The painting is compliments of the team. We all pitched in on it. I'd like to stay and chat, but I've got a practice I'm late for."

"I'm going to have to leave too, Dad," Finley said quickly. Suddenly, she felt as if she were imposing, and she longed to escape the scene. "I've got—some pictures to develop."

"Sure, sure, I understand." Mike kissed Finley's cheek, then shook Brady's hand. "Thanks. Tell the guys I really appreciate it." He turned to Alicia. "Do you have to run off, too?"

Alicia smiled. "I could stay long enough for a cup of coffee, I guess."

Mike returned her smile. "Great."

Finley edged from the room and Brady followed on her heels. Outside the office, Finley turned to him.

"Did you know that she knew him?"

"No." Brady shook his head. "Small world, isn't it?"

"Very small." Finley walked beside Brady. "They seemed to hit it off."

"Alicia's a nice lady. Are you going to the practice field with me?"

Finley's steps faltered. "What? Oh, no. I really do have some work to do." She glanced at him. "How's your hand? Tell the truth."

Brady placed his hands on her shoulders and leaned forward until he was eye level with her. "My hand is fine and that's the truth. Okay?"

His nearness sent a dizzy wave of pleasure through her, and Finley fought the urge to place her lips against his. His thumbs rubbed lightly against her collarbone before he pulled his hands from her shoulders. "Hey, what about—"

"Bryan!"

Finley turned to see Kristi bouncing toward them, her legs looking long and shapely. She was dressed in her cheerleading outfit. She tossed Finley a biting glance, then smiled demurely at Brady.

"You're supposed to take me to the practice field. Remember? *And* we have a lunch date."

"Excuse me." Finley shouldered past Kristi. Was he going to ask her out before Kristi's untimely arrival? Would she have accepted? Finley fumed at her own weakness. Of course she would have accepted. She stomped down the hall toward the photography lab and tried to shake the feeling of despair that threatened to engulf her. What chance did she have when Brady was surrounded by other women? Especially by Kristi! That woman seemed to be lurking around every corner!

6

The invitation was on green paper with gold lettering: "You're Invited To Brady's Mid-Season Bash!" Finley fingered the invitation thoughtfully, then opened it and read the date, time, and place. Brady's home on Saturday evening.

Should I go? Finley wondered. He's barely spoken to me the last several weeks. She leaned back in the rocking chair and let her gaze roam restlessly about the living room. Weekends filled with unpacking, cleaning, and sorting had finally paid off, and her apartment looked like a comfortable abode instead of a storage unit. She sighed, then looked at the invitation again. Brady's house. I've always wanted to see where he lives.

The doorbell chimed, and Finley placed the invitation on the coffee table and went to answer the door.

"Gena! Am I glad to see you." Finley stepped back to let Gena enter. "I've been cleaning this apartment until I feel like a drudge! How about some coffee?"

Gena laughed and stood for a moment, her gaze taking in the living room. "Looks great, Finley. Yes, coffee sounds nice. I'm glad I'm not disturbing you. As a matter of fact, I was doing some housework too, and I decided to drop everything and go visiting." She sat on the yellow couch and curled her legs under her.

Finley went into the kitchen and poured two cups of coffee. She set them on a tray with a pitcher of cream and a bowl of sugar and a plate of spice cookies, then went back into the living room. Gena sat straighter as Finley placed the tray on the coffee table.

"Ummm! Those cookies look good. Did you bake them?"

"Yes. Have one." Finley poured cream in her coffee and sat in the rocking chair.

"I see you got an invitation to Bryan's party. You're going, aren't you?"

"Are you?" Finley sipped her coffee.

"Of course. Jilly and I always go. Bryan throws one of these every year, you know."

"No, I didn't know. This is my first invitation." Finley eyed the invitation again. "Are they fun?"

"They're a ball!" Gena smiled and bit into one of the cookies. "These *are* delicious. Well, are you going to the party or not?"

Finley wrinkled her nose. "I guess so. I was surprised he invited me."

"Surprised? Why?"

"Because he hasn't been very friendly to me recently."

"Oh, well, that's understandable."

Finley gave Gena a sharp look. "What does that mean?"

Gena looked surprised. "He's been preoccupied with the games! Jilly's the same way. He's finally noticed that I'm around, but that's just because they have an off week. No games for ten days. That's why Bryan's having the party." Gena pursed her lips. "There's another reason for his aloofness, too, I think."

"What?"

Gena gave Finley a sly wink. "I think that Kristi raised a ruckus. She didn't like him spending so much time with you."

Finley raised surprised eyebrows. "*What* time? I've barely been around him!"

Gena laughed. "Well, he helped you move in here, and then you two went shopping."

"So what?!" Finley leaned back in her chair and rolled her eyes. "She must be awfully jealous-natured."

"When you don't have a very strong hold on a man, I guess you tend to be that way," Gena said softly.

Draining her coffee cup, Finley placed the cup on the tray and pondered Gena's statement. "So, you don't think it's that serious between Brady and Kristi?"

"Serious?" Gena laughed again. "No way. Kristi is just a distraction."

"I think *every* woman is just a distraction to Brady. He doesn't take anyone seriously."

"You sound bitter." Gena reached for another cookie. "Don't you think you're being hard on him?"

"No. He as much as admitted to me that women, *all* women, are playthings to him."

"Oh, I don't believe him," Gena said. "He just hasn't met the right woman."

Finley shrugged. "Maybe you're right. Anyway, Kristi shouldn't worry over me. She can have him as far as I'm concerned."

Gena wiped crumbs from her slacks. "Maybe she sees something different in his eyes when he looks at you."

Gena's words sent an enticing quiver through Finley. "Wh-what do you mean?" Finley asked in a whisper.

A knowing expression covered Gena's face. "I mean, let's be honest with each other, Finley. Are you *really* that immune to Bryan Brady's charms?"

Finley wiggled in the rocking chair, feeling suddenly exposed under Gena's probing gaze. Finally, she sighed, and shook her head. "You're right. I *try* to be flippant about him, but I *am* attracted to him, against my better judgement."

Gena smiled. "Why fight it? He's a nice guy. No! Really, he *is* nice. Give yourself a chance to get to know him and you'll see that I'm right."

Finley examined Gena for a few moments. "You like him a lot, don't you?"

"Beneath that playboy image is a nice man," Gena said. "Sure, he's had his wild flings, but he's more settled now." Gena laughed at Finley's disbelieving look. "He *is*. He's much more serious about his career these days, and believe it or not, he spends most of his evenings at home—alone—studying the playbook and the tendencies of other teams."

Finley poured herself another cup of coffee, then filled Gena's cup. "I've noticed that he's wrapped up in his job. He's had a tough season so far, physically."

"Yes, he has. He's hurting."

"Hurting?" Finley felt a stab of pain near the region of her heart at Gena's chilling statement. "So! He *is* injured!"

"Well." Gena frowned. "I don't know if he's *injured,* but Jilly says Bryan has been shaken up pretty badly in the past weeks." Gena shrugged, then smiled. "He's tough, like the rest of them. The important thing is that you get to know him and forget all that trash you've read about him. He's changed since the old days."

"Well, maybe you're right." Finley furrowed her brow. "Maybe I'll go to the party and woo him."

Gena laughed. "Watch out! When you start to woo the likes of Bryan, you'd better be ready for the consequences!"

"I can take care of myself," Finley said.

"Oh, I'm sure you can, but are you ready for the wagging tongues and the dagger looks you'll get from Kristi and the other ladies who have their sights set on Bryan?"

Finley set her cup down with a clatter. "I swear, I've never seen so many gossips in all my life! Football players are notorious for that, aren't they?"

Gena nodded. "You get a bunch of crazy guys together and they love to talk and kid around. And *they* say women gossip a lot!"

"Ha!" Finley shook her head. "I'm a ripe target for gossip, I guess, being the coach's daughter."

"That you are," Gena agreed. "Are you tough enough to take it?"

Finley squared her shoulders. "Sure! Bring on the lions!" Finley sobered slightly. "Gena, do you think Brady might be interested in me?"

"Hasn't he indicated that to you already?" Gena asked quietly.

"Y-e-s, but . . ."

Gena shook her head. "Don't dissect everything, Finley! Just let things happen!" She changed positions on the sofa. "Speaking of people being interested in other people, your dad seems to be seeing a lot of that artist, isn't he?"

Finley nodded. "Alicia? Yes, he likes her."

"She likes him, too. I can tell."

"Yes." Finley was quiet for a moment. "They seem to be pretty serious about each other."

"Any objections?"

Finley looked up to focus on Gena's curious expression. "No, not from me. I'd like for dad to have a lady friend. It would take some pressure off of me. I'm too old now to keep being his 'only' girl. You know?"

Gena smiled. "I hear you. I'm happy for the coach, too. I hope everything works out, for both of you." Gena glanced at her wristwatch. "Ooops! I've got to run. Thanks for the coffee and cookies."

Finley stood and walked to the door with Gena. "Thanks for the advice, Gena. What do people wear to Brady's bashes?"

"Evening clothes." Gena winked at her. "Look smashing!"

"Right." Finley bit her lip thoughtfully. "Can I go stag?"

"Stag?" Gena eyed Finley for a moment. "A girl like you can get a date."

"I'm not sure I *want* a date."

Gena touched Finley's shoulder. "Get a date and make Bryan *green* with jealousy!"

Finley tipped her head to one side. "You're cagey, Gena."

Gena giggled. "Honey, show me a woman who doesn't use tricks to catch her man and I'll show you a lonely woman."

Finley laughed. "See you at the party, Gena."

Closing the door, Finley crossed to the rocking chair and sat in it. She rocked for several minutes, her gaze locked on the invitation, her thoughts on Bryan Brady. The telephone bell pulled her from her deep thoughts, and she answered with some irritation.

"Finley? This is Rick Waverly. Am I disturbing you?"

"Rick! No, I was just—just cleaning my apartment."

"Oh, good. Listen, I called to ask if you'd like to go to Brady's party with me."

Finley strove to keep her voice even, though Rick's offer was a gift from heaven and her spirits soared. "How nice! I'd love to go with you, Rick."

"Really? Great! I'll pick you up at about seven thirty. How's that?"

"Fine. See you then." Finley replaced the receiver and smiled. Brady will *die* when he sees me with Rick, she thought, and a delicious exhilaration feathered through her. Gena's right. Game playing *can* be fun!

Bryan Brady's home was surrounded by crepe myrtle bushes that were at least ten feet high. Finley knew their blossoms would be red and pink, but fall was fading and winter was quickly approaching so no blooms rested in the branches. The leaves had begun to fall from the branches, creating a carpet around the house.

Finley walked with Rick to the front door and examined the polished oak and the large square of stained glass in it. The stained glass had a delicate tulip design with a border of roses. The house was Tudor and was located near the old depot. Finley was amazed, never having dreamed that Brady's house would look like this. Somehow, she had imagined it to be smaller and ordinary.

The door swung open, and Kristi stood on the threshold looking every bit the hostess. The blonde barely acknowledged Finley, but was quick to tuck her arm in Rick's and pull him inside.

"Ricky! I'm so glad you're here. Come in and let me take your coat and fix you a drink."

Rick shrugged out of his coat, then helped Finley shed hers. "Thanks, Kristi. Are we a little late?"

"Just on time! Bryan! Rick's here." Kristi guided Rick toward the bar, and Finley narrowed her eyes as she watched the blonde manhandle her date.

"Hey, Rick!" Brady extended a hand, then his gaze slid to Finley as Rick moved to put his hand across her shoulders. Brady's smile seemed strained. "Hi, Red. Glad to see you."

Finley felt a blush spread over her cheeks as Brady's gaze moved slowly over her deep violet evening gown. "Thanks for inviting us, Bryan."

Brady looked from Finley to Rick, then back to Finley. Now his smile vanished. "Well, fix yourself a drink and enjoy." He turned quickly and moved to a group at the other end of the spacious living room.

Finley accepted a cocktail and looked at her surroundings. The living room was decorated in muted browns and other earth tones. The furniture was rattan, and an Amazon parrot was chattering away in a wicker cage in one corner of the room. Finley smiled when she heard it call, "Four forty-two! Four forty-two! Hike! Hike!"

"I'm not surprised to see you with Rick."

Finley turned to find Gena at her side. "Why not?"

"He's had his eye on you for weeks! Hadn't you noticed?"

Finley shook her head. "No, but I'm glad he called."

"Yes. I noticed that Bryan was thrilled at seeing you with his backup."

Finley smiled, but felt no real accomplishment. "Where's Jilly?"

"He's fighting the crowds and getting me something to eat." Gena smiled and looked toward a crush of people near a long table. "I'm starved!"

"Hi, Gena!" Rick moved to stand beside Finley and he slipped an arm about her waist. "Sorry I got caught by Kristi, Finley. Would you like something to eat?"

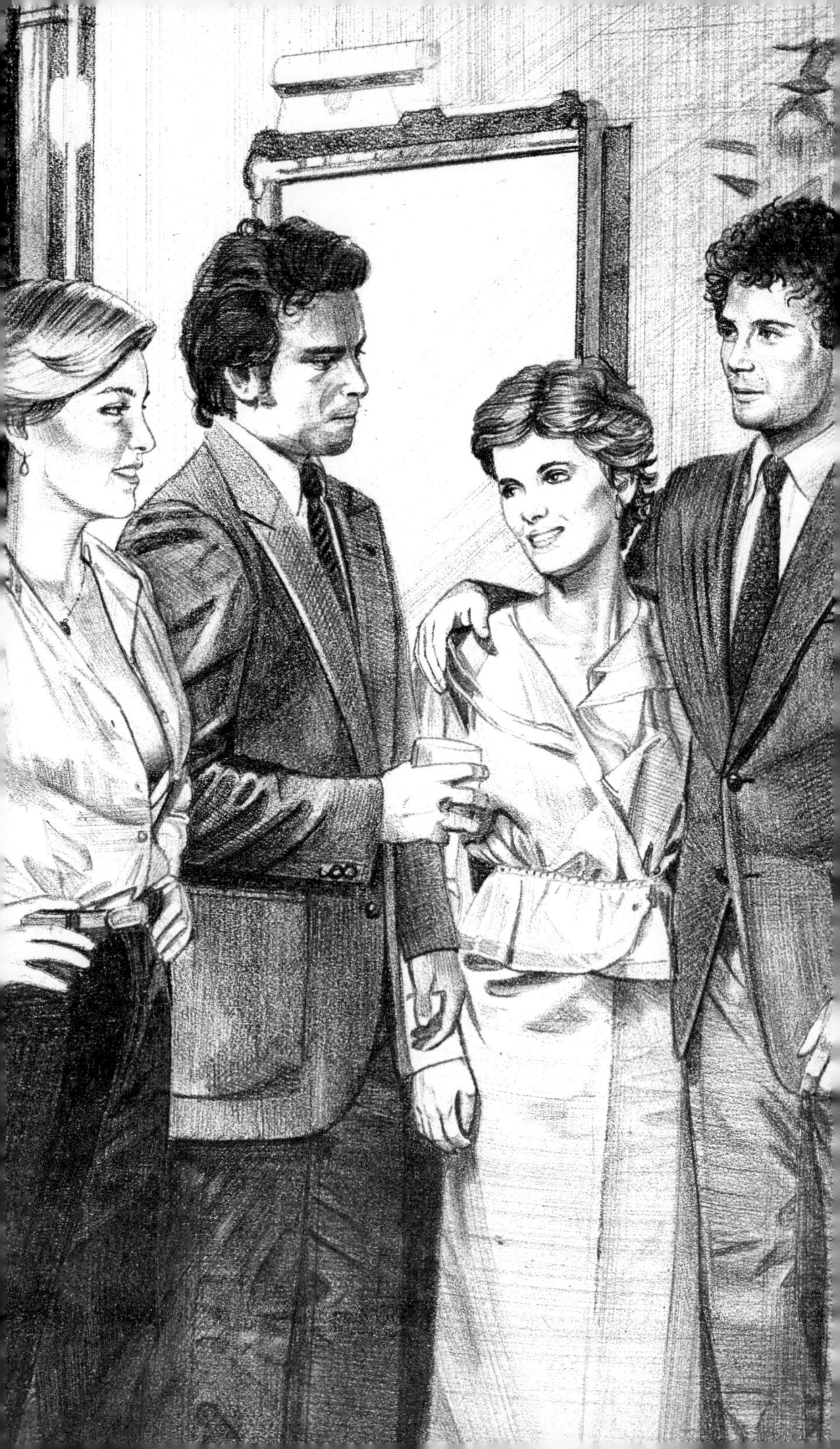

Finley nodded. "Would you mind?"

"No. Be right back." Rick brushed a kiss along Finley's cheek and whispered, "You look delicious!"

Finley smiled and was relieved when he left.

"Amorous devil, isn't he?" Gena's eyes danced.

"Too amorous. He's not my type, I'm afraid."

"I *know* your type and he's coming this way."

Finley tensed and turned to see Brady walking toward her. He was dressed in a dark suit that accented the width of his shoulders, a white shirt and dark tie completed the outfit, and to Finley, he seemed a little foreboding.

"Enjoying yourselves Finley, Gena?"

"I'm having a great time. Jilly and Rick are fetching us something to eat. I hope there's plenty."

"Don't worry." Brady's lazy gaze rested on Finley. "I didn't know you were seeing Rick."

"I see lots of people, Brady. I didn't think about reporting to you." Finley noted the quicksilver anger that glittered in his eyes.

"You misunderstand me, Finley. I don't *care* who you see. I was just making a casual comment." His gaze lifted and he smiled. "Here comes your food, ladies."

Finley turned to see Rick. He smiled and she tried to respond, but her misery was too acute. This is not working, she thought, as she watched Brady locate Kristi and plant a kiss on the blonde's waiting mouth. I don't *want* Rick's attentions and I'm stuck with them. She tried not to cringe when Rick's arm found her waist again. Again she looked toward Brady, and caught Kristi's gloating expression. Quickly, Finley turned away.

It was wrong of me to try and play games with Brady, she thought. After all, he's an expert at game playing. This whole evening has backfired.

Although she made a valiant attempt at having a good time, Finley found herself longing to escape Bryan Brady's home. When Rick was cornered by some fellow players,

Finley grabbed the opportunity and located the bathroom. She closed the door, locked it, and let the smile slip from her lips.

Halfheartedly, she repaired her makeup and tried to waste a few more minutes. She glanced at her wristwatch and sighed when she saw it was only ten o'clock. Can't ask Rick to leave the party now and take me home, she thought. Finally, she returned to the party. Rick was in deep conversation with Kevin and Jilly, and Gena was talking to some of the wives. Finley felt lost as she stood near the bar. She had a sudden urge to leave the party without Rick and make her apologies later.

"There's my girl!"

She turned to see her father and Alicia. Alicia was stunning in an ivory-colored evening gown that set off her dark tan.

"Oh, hello, Dad. Hi, Alicia."

"Finley?" Her father scrutinized her. "Are you feeling well?"

Finley sighed and gave up. "Not really. I—I've got an awful headache. Sinus, I think. I was just getting ready to call a cab. I don't want Rick to leave the party just because I'm not feeling so hot."

"That's too bad, Finley." Alicia stepped closer. "You sure it's only a headache?"

"Positive."

"Headache? Who has a headache?"

Finley frowned when Brady intruded in the circle.

"Finley," her father answered Brady. "She's going to have to call it an evening. I'll go call a taxi, honey."

"Taxi? What about Rick?" Brady raised a questioning brow.

"I—I don't want him to have to leave on my account." Finley looked to her father. "Would you call that taxi, Dad?"

"No, wait!" Brady rested a hand on Coach Malone's arm. "I have to go get some more ice. I'll take her home."

"No!" Finley shook her head and felt a real headache insinuate itself between her eyes. "It's out of your way and—"

"It's not that far."

"I will not hear of it!" Finley heard her voice rise, and she grimaced. "Really, I *want* to take a taxi!"

"What's going on?" Rick joined them and looked at Finley.

"Rick, I'm not feeling well and Dad's going to call me a taxi. I'm sorry."

"That's okay. I'm sorry you're feeling ill. I'll take you home." Rick rested a comforting arm about her shoulders.

"I've already offered her a ride, Rick, but she seems determined to ride home with a stranger."

Finley glared at Brady, then she turned to her father. "Dad, please?"

"Finley, please let me take you home?" Rick's voice was soft, but insistent. "I'll come back to the party. It's no trouble, really."

Finley sighed. "Very well. Thanks, Rick. Excuse us?" She stood on tiptoe and kissed her father's cheek. "Have fun and don't worry, it's just a headache." She shouldered past Brady and marched toward the foyer.

Rick caught up with her and helped her into her coat. The night was warm and starlit, and Finley was relieved to escape the confines of the party. Gratefully, she settled into the front seat of Rick's car and closed her eyes.

"Headache, or were you having a rotten time?"

Finley didn't open her eyes and decided to be truthful. "Both. Brady grates on my nerves."

Rick chuckled. "I caught those signals. What's between you two?"

"Nothing!" Now Finley's eyes snapped open and she looked at Rick. "What makes you think there's something between us?"

"Oh, just the way he looks at you. He didn't seem thrilled that I was your date." Rick glanced at her.

Finley shrugged. "Brady and I always seem at cross-purposes. Our chemistries clash."

"Are you sure about that?"

"Yes. I would think it was obvious." Finley straightened in the seat. "Let's not talk about Brady, okay?"

"Okay." Rick offered her a quick smile, then was silent.

At her apartment door, Finley kissed Rick lightly on the cheek, then turned her face away when he loomed closer.

"I'm really not feeling well, Rick. Sorry to spoil your evening."

"That's okay, Finley. We'll get together again soon."

Finley nodded and let herself into her apartment. She walked to her bedroom and sat on the bed with a muffled sob. Balling her hands into fists, she willed herself not to cry and was furious when a few tears trickled down her cheeks anyway.

"What an awful evening," she moaned. "But no more! I will *not* let that man spoil any more of my evenings or my days! He's not worth it!"

Her voice trembled in the empty room, and she thought of the party on the other side of the city. The throbbing in her temples increased, and she stood and went to the kitchen to find some aspirin.

7

The cold heart of winter seemed to have settled in upstate New York, and Finley guessed the temperature was pushing progressively down to the low teens. Following Brady's party, winter had gripped the nation in a cold fist, and a sharp-edged wind buffeted Finley as she stood on the sidelines and tried to forget that her fingers were numb beneath the wool gloves. She tried to concentrate on her work. Now, in the fourth quarter, Finley found that her thoughts were narrowing to that time when the game would end and she could seek shelter from the bitter cold.

Shivering, she readjusted the ski mask on her face and felt her eyes water as the chilling wind found them.

"Concentrate on the game and not on the cold!" she told herself, focusing her eyes on the middle of the frozen field.

The Wildcatters had the ball and they were one touchdown ahead of the New York team. Finley looked at the clock and was relieved to see that only five minutes remained. She stamped her feet and found she couldn't feel them inside her boots. What I'd give for a cup of hot chocolate and a blanket, she thought miserably. How can those guys even function out there?

Watching the games and listening to the comments around her had honed her spectator skills, and now she noted the formation of the defense and tensed when she recognized their intent to blitz the quarterback. Her gaze moved to

Brady, and out of the corner of her eye she saw Frank ready himself for the action. *Watch out, Brady!*

The ball was snapped, and Brady took three steps back before he planted his feet and searched for his receiver.

Too late!

Finley flinched as two defense men covered Brady and crushed him to the hard ground. But the ball had been thrown, and Jilly Jackson caught it in the end zone. The sidelined Wildcatters roared their approval and Finley watched Jilly prance and pose in the end zone before he spiked the football.

What a clown, Finley thought, before she returned her gaze to Brady. She sucked in her breath and felt the chilled air freeze her lungs when she saw that Brady was still on the turf and he wasn't moving. The trainer and his assistant were running onto the field and several of the Wildcatters were standing over Brady.

Get up! Get up! The words battered Finley's mind, and she realized she was holding her breath. She let it out and watched the cloud escape from her mouth. She squinted her eyes, ignoring the tears brought on by the cold air, and found herself trying to *will* Brady to move. Lifting her camera, she peered through the lens and saw the trainer push something under Brady's nose. He stirred, and she saw his helmet move from side to side. Finley breathed easier.

The trainer and the assistant heaved Brady to his feet and helped him to the sidelines. The team doctor met them there and they moved to the benches.

Finley crossed to them and watched as the doctor pulled Brady's helmet from his head. Despite the cold, Brady was perspiring and his eyes looked glassy and unfocused. The doctor stuck three fingers in front of Brady.

"Brady! How many fingers do you see?"

Brady grinned. "Four."

"How many?" The doctor moved his hand closer.

Brady squinted. "Oh. Two?"

Under her ski mask, Finley bit her lower lip and felt worry edge itself into her mind. Coach Malone stepped forward and concern was etched on his craggy face.

"What's the problem, doc?"

"I think he's got a concussion. I'm taking him in for X rays."

Coach Malone nodded. "Good idea. We're about to wrap this one up. I'll see you in a few minutes."

"Right." The doctor turned back to Brady. "Come on, son. The game's over."

"The game?" Brady blinked, but his eyes were still confused. "Did we score? What down is it?"

"Game's over. Come on, help me with him." The doctor motioned for the trainer and the two men helped Brady to his feet and walked slowly with him to the dressing rooms.

Finley watched until they were out of sight, then turned back to the game. The worry was still wrestling with her and now she found it completely impossible to concentrate on taking pictures. When the clock showed one minute, Finley gave up and began stowing away her camera. By the time the game had ended, Finley was outside the stadium searching for a taxi.

"Airport, please," she told the driver, then settled back in the seat. I'll be there two hours early, but I don't care. It will be warm there, she thought. I'll thaw out, have a cup of coffee, and get settled.

The airport was an oasis in a frozen world. Finley hurried to the coffee shop and sank into one of the booths. The coffee was warm, and she felt drowsy.

"You look worn out, honey."

Finley looked up at the waitress and smiled. "I am! My flight isn't due for another hour or two."

The waitress winked. "We're slow now. You take a snooze and I'll wake you in an hour." She nodded toward the ladies room. "There's a nice couch in there."

"Oh, heaven!" Finley paid for the coffee and went into the

ladies room. As promised, the couch was nice, and she fell asleep the moment her head rested on the cushion.

"Honey! Wake up. Your flight's been called. You *are* traveling with that football team, aren't you?"

Finley roused herself from the deep sleep and stared at the waitress. 'Yes. H-how did you know that?"

The waitress pointed to the overnight flight bag with the team's symbol stamped on its side. "By that. Did you sleep well?"

"And how!" Finley sat up and rubbed her eyes. "My flight's boarding?"

"Yes." The waitress placed her hands on her hips. "Your team won—this time!" She smiled. "Our boys really handed it to your quarterback, though."

Her words sent a chill through Finley. "What? Is he—?"

The waitress shrugged. "Don't know. I was listening to the game and the announcer said he had a concussion."

"Oh, yes." Finley stood and picked up her bags. "He's pretty tough. He's all right, I'm sure."

"Are you a photographer?" The waitress eyed Finley's camera case.

"Yes. Thanks again for waking me. That nap saved my life." Finley smiled at the waitress. "I got so chilled out there tonight I thought I would die!"

The waitress smiled. "Yeah, it's frigid out there now."

Finley thanked her again, then hurried to her gate. The players and managers were already on board, and Finley trotted down the aisle to take her seat next to Frank.

"Hey, princess! Where'd you disappear to?" Frank grinned at her and helped her stow her carry-ons.

"I came straight to the airport and found an angel in disguise." Finley smiled at his confusion. "A waitress showed me a heavenly couch in the ladies room and let me get in a quick nap. Frank, I was *freezing* out there tonight!"

Frank laughed. "Weren't we all?"

Brady's face floated before Finley's mind's eye, and she

leaned forward to see if he'd boarded the plane. His seat was empty. "Frank, where's Brady? The plane's taking off!"

Frank motioned to the back of the plane. "He's back there with the doc."

"The doctor?" Finley tried to see the back of the plane but couldn't. "What's wrong with him?"

Frank shrugged. "The doc says it's a concussion, and he's keeping an eye on him until he can examine him better in Tulsa."

"It's not serious, is it?"

"Don't know." Frank patted her hand. "Don't worry, sweetie. He's a big boy."

Finley settled in her seat, but found she couldn't get her mind off Brady. She yearned to walk to the back of the plane and talk to him, but resisted the urge. I'll see him when we land, she thought.

It was cold in Tulsa, too, but it was't snowing. Finley looked for Brady, but missed him. She cornered Jilly.

"Nice game, Jilly. Where'd they take Brady?"

Jilly gave her a sly smile. "To the exercise room. The doc wants to wrap his ribs and check on that bump on his head. Want me to drop you there?"

"Would you?"

"Sure, my car's here."

Finley followed Jilly to his silver Corvette Stingray and settled herself in the deep front seat.

"Jilly, how can you *afford* this monster?"

Jilly laughed. "Didn't you know? I'm a sports personality! A star!" He gave her a sidelong glance. "You're worried about old Brady, aren't you?"

"Yes, aren't you? I didn't think it was anything to worry about until I found out that the doctor was observing him on the flight home. It must be pretty bad. They might hospitalize him!"

"Naw!" Jilly shook his head. "When you've got a slight concussion, the doc just likes to keep an eye on you for a few hours and make sure you don't do something stupid. You see, Brady's a little out of it now." Jilly chuckled. "I don't even think he knows the game's over."

Finley gasped. "That's terrible!"

"Now, now, don't get excited." Jilly gave her an encouraging wink. "It's *normal.* He'll snap out of it. I've been in the same boat. By morning, he'll be fit as a fiddle."

"I-I hope so." Finley chewed on her lower lip and tried to believe Jilly's words.

"Here we are. Want me to wait?"

"No. I can walk home from here. Thanks, Jilly!" Finley scrambled from the car and trotted to the exercise room behind the stadium. The bowels of the stadium were silent and dark except for a pool of light at the exercise room. Finley walked into the room and found it empty.

She started to call out when she heard Kristi's voice. Quickly, Finley melted back into the shadows of the corridor and looked into the lighted room. Kristi came into view with Brady.

"You sure you don't want me to stay?"

"No, you go on." Brady kissed her cheek. "I'm okay."

"You sure? I'll stay."

"No, you go on to that party at Kevin's and have a good time. I'm going home and get some shut-eye."

"W-e-ll, okay." Kristi gave him a quick kiss on the lips. "You look awful, Bryan."

"Thanks. See you later."

Kristi hurried from the room and Finley pressed farther back in the shadows, her back plastered against the wall. Kristi marched past, and Finley breathed a relieved sigh. Footsteps sounded along the corridor, and Finley peered through the darkness and saw the flash of a white coat. The doctor.

The doctor went into the exercise room. "Ah, Bryan. How do the ribs feel?"

"Okay. Can I go home now?"

"Yes. The X rays show a slight concussion, and I don't

want you to be alone. I'll have my assistant go home with you."

"No." Brady shook his head, grimaced, and placed a hand on the back of his neck. "Kristi will be there."

"You sure?" The doctor glanced over his shoulder. "I thought she just left."

"She did. She's—she's going to my place. I'm going to meet her there."

Can't he see that Brady's lying? Finley wondered. He sent Kristi to a party!

"Well, as long as you're not alone," the doctor said, rubbing his chin thoughtfully. "I want someone with you in case you get sick during the night. That medication I gave you could result in a queasy stomach." The doctor reached into his pocket and brought out a bottle of tablets. "Take two of these in the morning and come in here tomorrow for a whirlpool treatment. If you need me, call me."

"Will do, doc. Thanks." Brady took the pills and shoved them into his coat pocket.

"You'll be sore in the morning, and you'll probably have a whopper of a headache."

"I can handle it. Good night." Brady shook the doctor's hand and strolled from the room.

"Bryan!" The doctor waited for Brady to face him. "Take a taxi home. Don't drive."

"Okay." Brady turned and walked past Finley's hiding place.

Finley wrestled with whether or not to inform the doctor that Brady was going home to an empty house, then decided not to. Instead, she followed Brady from the stadium and watched as he headed for his car. An irritated sigh escaped her. *The fool!*

"Hey, Brady!" She ran toward him and placed a hand on his arm.

Glazed blue eyes bore into hers. Brady blinked once, twice. "Yeah? Who are you?"

Alarms sounded in Finley's mind and she tightened her

grip on his arm. "Brady! It's me! Finley! Don't you know me?"

Recognition filtered into his glassy gaze. "Oh, Red. Hi." He looked around him. "What are you doing here? You should be at the party." He looked at her again and that glassy glaze iced his eyes again. "The game *is* over, isn't it?" He laughed. "Yeah, it's over. We're home, aren't we?"

"Yes. We're home. I don't want to go to the party. I'm driving you home. Get in on the other side."

"Driving me home?" Brady massaged his neck again. "No, you go to the party and tell the guys I'm okay. I can drive."

"Didn't you hear the doctor?" He was turning away from her, and Finley pulled on his arm to get his attention. "The doctor said you were *not* to drive. Now, get in on the other side!" She pulled at him again.

"Okay, okay!" He jerked from her grasp. "Who asked you here? You're not my mother!"

"Thank heavens for that!" Finley climbed into the car and held out her hand to him. "The keys?"

He dropped the keys into her hand. "You know where I live?"

"I was there at a party once. Remember?"

"Oh, yeah." He leaned his head back against the seat. "My head feels like it's splitting open."

"You just relax. You've had quite a day and night."

"What time is it?"

His words were slurred, and Finley glanced at him with a tinge of apprehension. "It's almost eleven o'clock."

"What was the score of the game?"

"It was twenty-one to seven. We won."

"Did I finish the game?"

"No. Rick played the last few minutes, but you threw the last touchdown pass."

"Oh, good. I don't remember that."

"I'm not surprised. Right after you released the ball two

mountains from the other team crashed down on you. Is there a bump on your head?"

Gingerly, he felt the crown of his head and winced. "Yes. I guess that accounts for my headache."

In the dim light of the car, Finley could see the pallid skin around his eyes, but it was the bright flush of color on his cheeks that disturbed her. Fever? She reached out a hand and laid the back of it against his cheek. He edged away from her.

"You have a fever."

"Do I?" He felt his forehead. "Funny, I'm shivering."

"Shivering?" Finley steered his car into his driveway and cut the engine. "I need to get you inside and into bed."

"Sounds lovely." He gave her a wicked wink before leaving the car and walking, not quite steadily, to the front door.

Inside, he headed for the stairs and climbed them slowly. Finley followed him and wondered if he'd make it. Finally, he reached the landing and veered to the left. He glanced over his shoulder and smiled.

"Still with me? Come into my parlor." He swept an arm in the direction of a room at the end of the short hall. Finley preceded him and gazed appreciatively at the decor.

The bedroom was large, taking up most of the second floor. A massive waterbed was in the center of the room, and a gold spread covered it. The windows were lattice work, stained glass in greens, golds, and browns. One entire wall was mirrors, and Finley saw that each was a door, presumably opening to closets.

"Very impressive." She turned to find that he was stumbling toward the bathroom. "Need any help?"

"No. I've been going to the bathroom by myself for years, thank you."

Finley didn't miss the iciness in his voice, and she balled her hands into fists and went to sit in an emerald green chair in the corner of the room. She watched as he closed the bathroom door and fury seized her when she heard him lock it.

What does he think? she wondered. Does he expect me to follow him in there? After a few minutes she heard the shower, and she hoped he didn't fall. He seemed awfully dizzy-headed, she thought. The fool doesn't know how weak he is right now.

Restless, Finley rose from the chair and crossed to the bureau. She ran her fingers along the smooth wood and let her eyes take in the various pieces of jewelry scattered on the top of the bureau. A small gold necklace. Several pairs of cuff links. A wristwatch. Two or three rings, one from Notre Dame. Her breath caught in her throat when she saw a bracelet—a woman's bracelet.

Slowly, her fingers closed around it and she lifted it to examine the gold charm that dangled from the links. The word leapt at her: "Kristi."

Finley dropped the bracelet and turned from the bureau. Does Kristi stay here with him? Would she return here after the party? Quickly, Finley crossed to the wall of mirrors and opened one door after the other. Relief washed through her when the closet revealed only Brady's clothing.

"Do you like my tailor or are you simply nosy?"

She spun in the direction of the voice and found Brady standing near the bed. He wore nothing but a blue bathrobe, and Finley caught the heady scent of soap and after-shave lotion.

"I—I was just—"

"Never mind." He sat on the bed and massaged his neck. "Now that I'm safely delivered you can leave."

"I'll fix you a cup of warm milk before I leave. It will relax you."

"Put some brandy in it and I'll drink it." He lay back on the bed and it rippled beneath his weight.

"I don't think you should mix liquor with those pills the doctor gave you."

He didn't answer, and Finley shrugged and went downstairs to the kitchen. She poured milk into a pan and put it on the stove. While waiting for the milk to warm, she thought of the man upstairs.

I don't like the color of his skin, she thought. And he's got a fever, but he's shivering. Is that an aftereffect of the medication or—? What?! She stamped one foot and wished for medical advice. Maybe if he doesn't get better before I leave, I'll phone the doctor.

The milk bubbled, and she poured it into a mug and went upstairs. The bathrobe was in a pool on the floor and Brady was in bed, the covers clutched under his chin.

"Here's your milk." Finley set it on the bedside table. "Brady! You're shaking!" She put a hand to his forehead and the skin there was hot and clammy. "I'm going to call the doctor."

"No!"

Feverish fingers curled around her wrist and his eyes seemed to blaze. Finley gasped when he pulled her to sit on the bed.

"Don't call the doctor," he whispered, enunciating each word as if she were a child who had trouble understanding.

"But, I'm afraid! I don't know what to do!"

"Just get me another blanket and let me drink that milk. Did you put some brandy in it? No. You wouldn't." He reached for the cup. His teeth chattered against the edge as he drank its contents.

With some trepidation, Finley stood and looked down at him. "Where are the blankets?"

He nodded toward the mirrored wall. "In there, up on the top shelf. Can you reach them?"

She opened one of the doors. "Yes, just barely." She stretched and yanked down a couple of wool blankets, then spread them on the bed. "I still think I should call the doctor."

"No." He set the empty mug on the table. "The doctor will

tell the coach and the coach will put me on the injured list. I don't want that because I'm going to be fine tomorrow. I just need . . . some . . . sleep."

Finley caught the slurring words and she watched him snuggle deep into the bed and close his eyes. His breathing became slow and heavy and Finley moved to his side, alarm spreading through her.

"Brady? Bryan!"

In response, he turned onto his side and moaned. "Cold. I'm . . . so . . . cold." The blankets quivered.

"Oh, Brady!" Finley looked about the room, as if she'd find some miracle there. Doubt nagged at her as she began pacing the bedroom, her gaze returning repeatedly to the man who shivered in the bed. Again she thought of telephoning the doctor, but she recalled his adamant protest and she knew he'd never forgive her if she disobeyed him.

What if I called Dad? She stopped pacing for a moment, then shook her head. No. Brady would be furious! He's right. Dad *would* put him on the injury list. But shouldn't he? Brady *is* injured! No. It's not my decision to make.

She went to the bed and looked at Brady. His breathing was shallow and light now, and when she touched his shoulder, his skin felt sticky. Finley moaned.

"We'll pass. Cover me! Ready! Hike!"

His voice was hoarse and Finley stepped back. Oh, God! Now he's delirious! Helplessness consumed her. I'll call Jilly and Gena!

She marched to the telephone and quickly dialed the number. The telephone rang twelve times before she replaced the receiver. They're at the party, she thought. How can they party? I'm exhausted! Weak-kneed, she sat on the bed and felt it slosh beneath her. She smiled at the sensation. I've never slept in a waterbed before, she mused as her fingers traced the gold and green patterns of the sheet. It's strange!

Brady moved restlessly and murmured and Finley stood, her eyes wide.

"Cold out here . . . so cold . . ." He shivered and pulled the blankets closer to him.

"Oh, Brady, what am I going to do with you?" Finley's gaze rested on the bathrobe at her feet, and a thought wormed its way into her troubled mind. Body heat? Would that help?

Without thinking further about it, Finley stripped off her slacks and shirt and wrapped the huge bathrobe about her, then she slipped into bed beside Brady. She put her arms around his shivering shoulders and he mumbled something. Then, like a half-frozen animal seeking the warmth of the sun, he moved closer to her until he had pressed the length of his body against hers.

"So warm . . . so warm . . ." He pressed his face into the curve of her neck and his breath was warm, but light.

Finley sighed and held him close. Before sleep covered her in a toasty blanket, she said a silent prayer for the man she held in her arms.

It was the feeling of a heavy hand on her stomach that woke her. Finley's eyelids fluttered up and she gazed, dazed, at the ceiling.

Where am I?

The sound of regular breathing stirred her, and she glanced at the mass of sandy hair resting on her shoulder. She stiffened, then relaxed. Brady.

Carefully, she wiggled from his hold and slid from the bed. She leaned over him and was relieved to see a normal coloring to his skin. He was breathing deeply now and he was warm, no longer shivering and clammy. She straightened and looked at the clock on the table. Seven o'clock.

Wrapping the bathrobe tighter, she walked to the window and pushed it open so that she could see the morning. Sunlight filtered through a thick mist and the air was cold and bracing. Finley shivered and started to close the window, then she saw a car pull into the driveway behind Brady's car.

She froze and waited to see Kristi emerge from the car. Still wearing the same outfit as last evening, Kristi stretched and yawned. Then her gaze lifted and she stared at Finley.

Still drugged by sleep, Finley stared back at the surprised woman. For a moment, she almost called out "Good morning!" but the shock, then anger, on Kristi's face stopped her. Awareness flooded through her, and Finley placed a hand to her mouth.

What must she think? I'm here at Brady's in *his* bathrobe, standing in *his* bedroom! I have to go down and explain!

But Kristi's face was hard with hatred now, and she whirled and climbed back into her car. Tires screamed on the pavement as she backed the car out of the driveway and sped down the street.

"Oh, dear." Finley closed the window and turned to stare at Brady. "Now I've done it!"

Brady moved under the covers and stretched out an arm. His hand quested for a moment, then lay limp on the sheet. Finley moved to stand by the bed, and a loving smile captured her mouth as she looked down at him.

Dark lashes rested against his cheeks, and his mouth was slack and vulnerable. A nasty bruise was visible just under his left eye. He looked like a little boy who'd just lost his first fight.

Finley chided herself. There you go again, thinking of him as a little boy, and you *know* what happened last time you thought like that! The memory sent a quiver through her as she recalled the sweet pressure of his lips on hers.

She crossed her arms and tilted her head in a thoughtful pose. He *is* vulnerable now. He's weak and he's hurt. She shrugged and slid back under the covers. Immediately, his arm came to rest across her stomach and he pulled her to him. Finley tensed, wondering if he were awake. No, his breathing was regular and deep. Does he imagine *I'm* Kristi? The thought was too painful, and she shoved it aside. Enjoy, she thought. This is a chance of a lifetime! She snuggled closer to him and slept.

• • •

A muscular, rough leg snaked up along Finley's leg and a firm mouth covered hers.

Sucking in her breath, she fought, her arms flailing and her legs kicking, before she opened her eyes to see the glitter of cobalt blue eyes. Amusement sparkled in those eyes before Brady pushed himself from Finley and grinned. He propped his head in one hand and chuckled.

"I don't know how you got here or what we've been doing—I'm just very grateful."

"We haven't been doing anything—except sleeping!" Finley pulled the bathrobe close and inched from him. His arm shot out to wrap about her waist. "Stop it! You're sick and you shouldn't be—"

His mouth covered hers in a hard, quick kiss. "Who's sick? Me?" Again his lips captured hers and this time stayed to taste and tease. His arm tightened about her waist, and he pulled her to him.

Finley squirmed for a moment, but his mouth was too intoxicating and she ceased her struggling. His teeth nibbled at her bottom lip before he moved his mouth to kiss her earlobe, and now his hand was tracing lazy circles on her stomach. Roughly, he pushed the bathrobe from her shoulders so that his fingers could caress her skin. Finley trembled under his touch and wrapped her arms about his strong neck, pulling his head to her so that she could kiss him.

A flowering warmth grew in her stomach to blossom down her legs, and she pressed closer to him, arching her back so that every inch of her was touching him. He was like wildfire, and the feel of him sent the rest of the world into a void, leaving only the touch, taste, and smell of him.

"Finley, I'm so glad you're here . . . so glad . . ." His breathing was short and his breath whispered on her neck as his lips traced a path of fire to her shoulder.

Finley felt herself slipping, writhing, into a passionate funnel. She held to him, silently begging him to escort her through this new and terrifying world. Part of her trembled

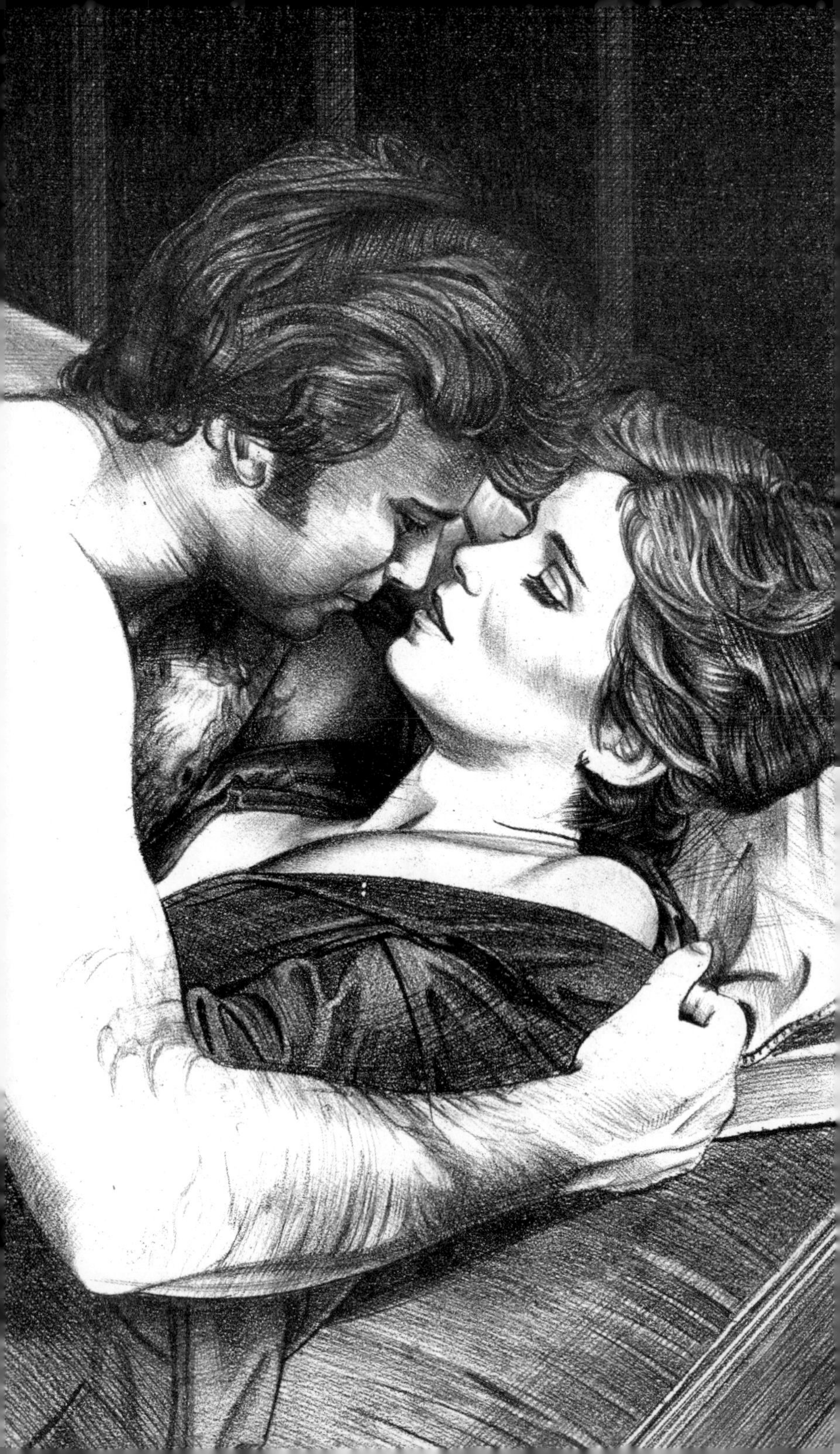

on the brink of the new experience, while another part of her held her to the world she knew—the safe, secure world of rationality.

While his hands roamed her body and his kisses became more drugging, pulling her deeper, deeper into the funnel, that rational part of her tugged at her mind until it finally showed her the trump card. A vision of an angry, vindictive Kristi Sinclair flashed before her, and Finley froze as she recalled the earlier incident.

Frantically, she pushed at Brady's broad shoulders, finally pounding him with her fists until his mouth left hers and his eyes focused on her flushed face.

"Kristi was here earlier!" Her voice sounded weak and unfamiliar.

"What?" He blinked, then pushed himself from her. "When?"

"Earlier this morning. She drove up and saw me standing there, by the window!"

"What?!" He looked at the place by the window and shook his head. He grimaced and placed a hand on the top of his head. "Wow! What hit me?"

"Brady!" Finley scrambled from the bed, her hands pulling the robe back onto her shoulders and tying the sash. "She—she thinks I spent the night with you!"

"Well, you did, didn't you?" He was rolling his shoulders and pain was evident in his face.

"Yes, but not like that! I was worried about you—you have a concussion!"

Again, he touched the top of his head. "So I gathered." He looked toward the bathroom, then looked back at Finley. "Since you seem to be wearing my bathrobe and I would like to take a shower, would you mind handing me something to put on or would you like to see *all* of the merchandise?"

Finley felt her face grow hot, and she rushed to the closets and rummaged through them until she found a maroon bathrobe. She tossed it to him, then turned her back. The waterbed sloshed as he rose, and Finley kept her eyes fastened to the floor for a moment. When she lifted her gaze, she found herself staring at his reflection in the closet door mirrors. He was closing the robe and fastening the belt, but in that brief second Finley caught a glimpse of powerful thighs, a flat, muscled stomach, and a broad chest covered by reddish-blond hair. A tremor skirted through her and she took a deep breath.

"You can turn around now." He moved toward the bathroom. "Let me shower and then we'll talk. Okay?" He paused and placed his hands on his hips, then twisted his body carefully. He grimaced. "I *know* I played football yesterday because I feel like a ninety-year-old man today."

"Don't you remember the game?" Finley touched his arm and she felt her eyes widen in concern.

"Yes. I just don't remember finishing the game." He patted her hand. "Make some coffee, will you?"

She nodded and watched him enter the bathroom and close the door. Quickly, she stripped off the bathrobe and put on her clothes. She ran a comb through her tousled hair and tried not to think of Brady or the events of the past twenty-four hours.

However, the memories consumed her while she waited in the kitchen for the coffee to brew, and she sat at the kitchen table and rested her face in her hands. She could feel the heat of her blush.

How could I have done that? she wondered. How could I have put on his robe and slept with him? Am I losing my mind? Why, when he woke up this morning he must have thought that I was offering myself to him! The thought sent a new wave of remorse through her and she moaned. *And Kristi knows.* Something akin to panic filled her, and she shuddered. That woman could make trouble, and I've put a loaded revolver in her hands!

But nothing happened! Finley folded her arms and buried her face in them on the table top. I was concerned about him and he was shivering and—and—Oh, who's going to believe that?! But, it's true!

"Can't be *that* bad, Finley."

His voice halted her mental torture and she lifted her head to find him by the counter, pouring two cups of coffee. "Do you take it black?"

"Cream and sugar, please."

Finley watched as he prepared the coffee. He was dressed in jeans and a red plaid flannel shirt. Scuffed cowboy boots added another inch to his tall frame. He looked much better. Only the bruise under his eye and a hint of pain in his eyes told her of the beating he had taken yesterday. He hadn't shaved, and a dark stubble covered the lower part of his face.

"Here you go," he said, placing the coffee before her. He sat opposite her and pinned her with a serious stare. "Okay! Now, you say that Kristi saw you standing by my bedroom window?"

"Yes." Finley took a deep breath. "I woke up and decided to get up and stretch my legs. I was standing by the window looking out at the morning when Kristi drove up. I—I wasn't thinking or I would have stepped back into the room, but I just stood there!" Finley shook her head and sipped the hot coffee. "She looked up and saw me and—oh, Brady, you should have seen her face! She was furious!"

Now he smiled. "Yes, I imagine she was just that."

"There's no telling what she might do—who she might tell!" Finley gasped and covered her mouth with her hand as a burning thought branded her.

"What?" Brady reached across the table and covered her hand. "What's wrong?"

Slowly, Finley let her hand slide from her mouth. "Brady! She might even tell my dad!"

"The coach?" Brady shook his head. "No, she wouldn't do that."

The shrill ring of the telephone made them both jump, and Brady threw Finley a sheepish look.

"Don't get excited! My telephone rings all the time, especially the day after a game." He patted her hand and went to answer the telephone.

Finley drank her coffee and strained to catch Brady's telephone conversation. All she could hear was the baritone rumbling of his voice, and she fought the urge to leave the kitchen and listen to his discussion.

He returned and gave her the thumbs-up sign. "It was the doctor making sure I was okay and that I'd be in today for treatment. See? Nothing to worry about."

"But I *am* worried! You know Kristi!"

"Yes. Yes, I do." He sat at the table again and finished his coffee in two gulps. "She wouldn't do anything stupid. She knows I wouldn't have anything else to do with her if she went blabbing to your dad. Besides, you said nothing happened."

"It didn't! But who'd believe that?" Finley chewed on her lip a moment and felt fury lick at her when Brady laughed.

"Actually, I'd just as soon no one knows that nothing happened. I have a reputation to think of, you know."

"Well, what about *my* reputation?!" Finley balled her hands into fists and glared at him.

"Easy, Red. I'm kidding." He gave her a small smile, then poured himself another cup of coffee. "I'll talk to Kristi today and get this whole thing ironed out."

The doorbell chimed and Brady rolled his eyes. "It's like Grand Central Station here this morning." He rose and went to answer the door.

This time Finley followed him, but stayed back a little. She hated the feeling of shame that crept over her and she reminded herself that she'd done nothing wrong. She'd just used bad judgment.

"Coach! What are you doing here?"

Shame threatened to choke Finley as she stared at her father. His face was ashen and his eyes seemed to burn her where they touched.

"I want to talk—to *both* of you."

Finley shivered from the ice that coated her father's words.

8

Finley paced the length of Bryan's living room and winced as her stomach muscles tightened until she was sure she might be sick at any moment. Her nerves seemed to quiver like plucked violin strings as her gaze kept returning to the closed study door across the hall from the living room.

What's going on in there? her mind screamed. What can they be discussing for so long? Surely Dad *knows* this is all just a misunderstanding! She glanced at the clock on the mantle and was surprised to see that only thirty minutes had elapsed since Brady and her father had retired to the study to discuss some "business."

She recalled her hasty explanation to her father about why she was at Brady's and what had transpired last night. Although he had nodded and muttered something about how he trusted her and knew she wouldn't do anything stupid to jeopardize her career, not to mention Brady's, there was something in his eyes that bothered Finley. She sighed and tried to pinpoint the element she had seen in her father's steady gaze. Disappointment? Anxiety? No. It was something that was foreign to her.

She stifled a gasp when the study door swung open and her father and Brady emerged from the room. Finley walked to her father and knew that her face was pale and her expression was pleading.

"Dad, is everything okay? I mean . . . I . . ."

Mike Malone kissed her cheek. "Don't worry, honey. It's not the end of the world." He glanced at his wristwatch. "I've got to go. See you later?"

Finley nodded, unable to speak around the lump of emotion lodged in her throat. Suddenly, she felt weak and tired as she watched her father climb into his car and drive away. She turned back to Brady and found that he was slumped in a chair in the living room.

"What did you and Dad talk about?" Finley walked slowly into the room and examined Brady's scowl.

"We talked about things like team effort and attitudes."

Finley sighed. "Can't you be more specific?"

The directness of his gaze sent a current of apprehension through Finley and she crossed her arms and moved back a step or two. His eyes were a bright sky blue as he surveyed her for a moment, then looked away.

"I think we should get married, Finley."

"To each other!" Finley swallowed the hysterical giggle that rose in her throat. She felt her eyes widen and she placed a hand to her mouth to hide the smile there.

"Yes. To each other."

His solemn expression chased the merriment from her and she felt her mouth tighten into a straight line against her fingertips. She removed her hand from her mouth and gave him a cool stare.

"Is *that* what you and Dad decided? Don't you think it's a trifle dramatic? A bit Victorian?" She moved to stand by the fireplace, her back resting against the mantle. "I think you're overreacting. This is the twentieth century! Women have the right to do whatever they please, and that *includes* keeping company with men overnight!"

Brady's eyes twinkled. "You sure have changed your tune. Just a few minutes ago you were worried about what people might say about this whole thing."

"Well, I've given it some thought and I've come to the

conclusion that most people really don't care about such things. It's nobody's business."

Brady rolled his shoulders. "You know, Finley, I don't believe a word you're saying. You expect me to believe that you wouldn't mind if the team and managers started gossiping about you and me?"

Finley shrugged. "It wouldn't last long. They'd tire of the topic very quickly."

"Not quickly enough, I'm afraid."

His tone was flat and uncompromising, and Finley felt herself losing ground. "Brady, you're not serious about this! We can't get married! We don't love each other and—and you wouldn't be faithful to me."

"Who says?"

Finley laughed, although she found nothing humorous in the situation or the proposal. "I don't believe this! Are you telling me that you *do* love me and that you *want* to spend the rest of your life married to me?

He didn't answer for several moments. Finley felt an odd sensation curl in her stomach. She wanted to scream at him and demand an answer, but one part of her mind cringed at the prospect of him rejecting her completely.

"No, I'm not saying that I love you."

His answer seemd to stab at her and Finley felt a dull pain throb in her temples. She moved to sit on the couch and wondered at the desolation that seemed to fester in her soul.

"What I *am* saying is that I find you . . . attractive and good company. I care for you, Finley, and I don't want to put you through something painful and destructive." He leaned forward, resting his elbows on his knees, and pinned her with a frank stare. "You're right about attitudes being more lenient today concerning the conduct of adults in adult situations, but we're in a different position. We both work for a football team, and that's akin to a fraternity. Everything that happens is everybody's business. Gossip can be a vicious, destructive weapon when it's placed in the right hands and at the right time."

Finley shook her head. "I'm not following you."

"Okay." He sighed and ran one hand through his hair. "You haven't been in this business very long, but I have and I know how this kind of thing can affect a team."

"What kind of thing?" Finley heard her voice rise with irritation and she forced a softer tone. "I'm not the first woman who—who's stayed here. You have a very lively reputation where women are concerned. No one has *ever* accused you of being—being a monk!"

A derisive smile curved his full lips. "No, no, that's true, but you're forgetting one important point." He paused, letting the silence settle like a thick, choking fog in the still room. "You are the coach's daughter and I'm the team's quarterback and captain."

She gave him a questioning look, lifting her eyebrows in a silent plea.

"Finley, that's dynamite stuff for gossips and folks with a yen for verbal abuse. What's more, I feel like we've placed a barrier in my relationship with the coach."

"What?" Finley saw the sadness filter into his eyes and her heart thumped against her ribs. "Is Dad really upset about this?"

Brady sighed and leaned back in the chair. "Upset? I think he's disappointed and he's dreading—just as I am—the inevitable problems and tension this will evoke." Brady spread his hands in a helpless gesture. "You have to understand that the team is at a very critical point right now. We're gunning for the title and the team *must* stay together in all respects. Something like this will cause divisions, just like the division I feel now with the coach."

"So, what you're saying is that if this had happened with anyone else besides me, it wouldn't be so traumatic," Finley said.

"Yes." Brady closed his eyes and his face looked weary.

"Can't you imagine the hateful things that will be said? Brady's hustling the coach's daughter so that he'll have an inside track. The coach's daughter is just like the rest of the football groupies."

"Stop!" Finley placed her hands over her ears and squeezed shut her eyes. The words battered at her and she felt hot tears form in her eyes.

"I'm sorry, honey." Brady's voice was soft and caressing and he moved to sit beside her on the couch. He placed an arm about her shoulders. "I was just making a point. Accusations like that will hurt me, too. I have to *lead* the team, not divide it into factions of jealousy and mistrust. The coach knows this situation is explosive and can ruin the team's attitude and that's why he's worried. He *trusts* you to make the right decisions and to do the right thing, Finley. It's just that he knows human nature—the darker side of human nature—and how it can eat away at people and at goals like a cancer."

"But—but how can marrying me stop the gossip? Everyone will just say that we got caught redhanded and we married in a hurry so that Dad wouldn't have a fit! Or—or they'll say that I'm pregnant!" Finley felt her eyes water as the horror of the thought tore at her mind.

"No. It won't work that way." Brady wiped the tears from her cheeks with his thumbs and gave her a warm smile. "We'll fly to Las Vegas and get married and tell everyone that we were married *before* the New York game. Who will know the difference besides us and the coach?"

Finley leaned away from him and stared at him in shock. "You mean—cover up and lie about this? No one will believe that we got married before the New York game! Why, we were hardly *speaking* before the game—and why would we keep our marriage a secret?"

Brady shrugged. "What secret? We just didn't want anyone to know until after the game, since the New York game was so important to the team. We'll say we were going to

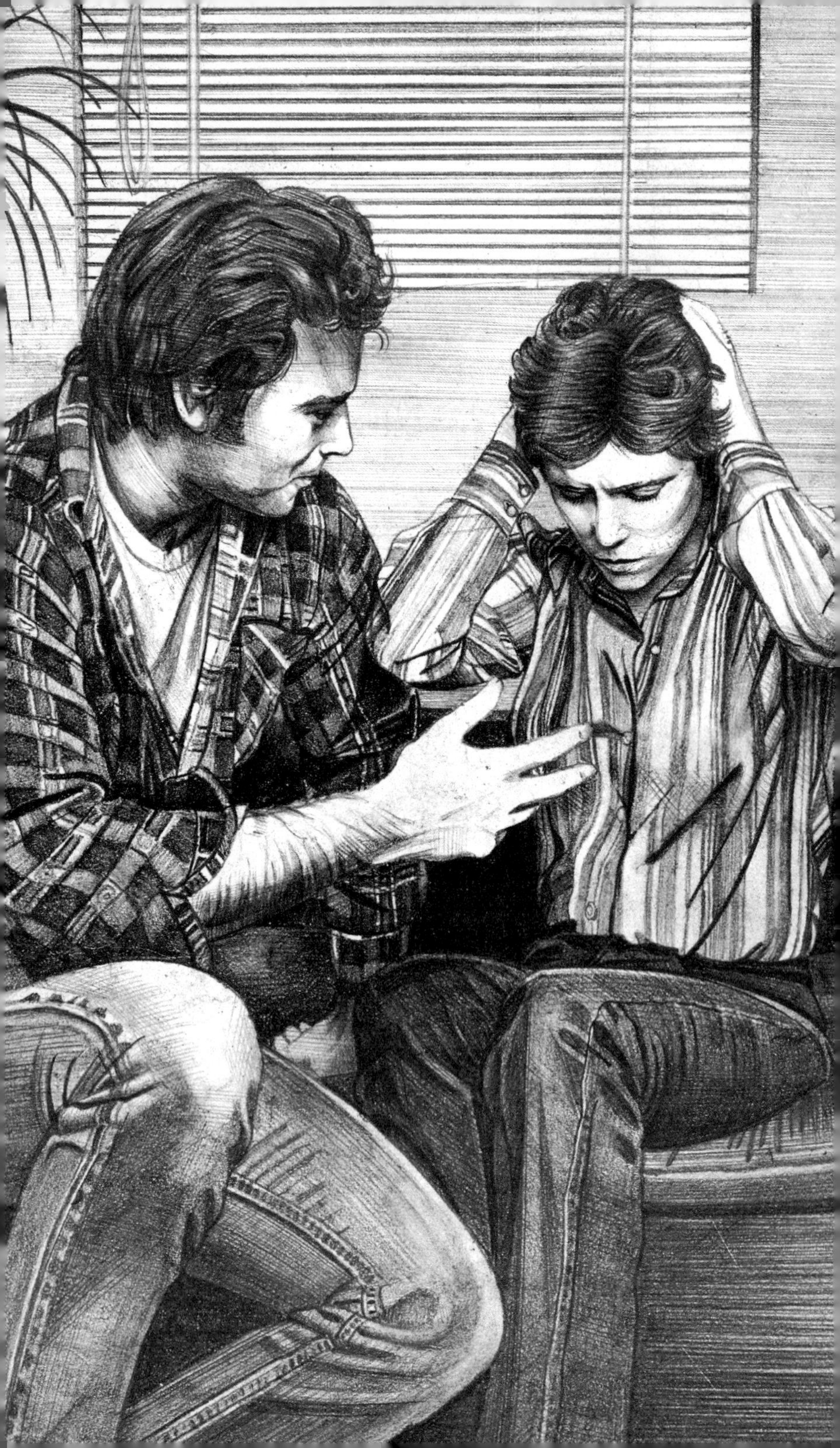

announce our marriage at Kevin's party, but my concussion ruined the idea."

Finley shook her head. "My, my. You sound like you've had a lot of practice at this sort of thing."

"I just have a devious mind."

"And what about the future? How long do we stay married? How long can we keep up the charade?"

"For as long as we have to," Brady said. "At least until we win the championship, then we'll get a quiet divorce or—or whatever's best."

"Divorce." Finley hated the taste and sound of the word and she felt her face tighten with revulsion. "You make it sound like an everyday occurence."

"Well, isn't it?"

"Not to me! None of my family has ever divorced!" Finley tried to smother the anger that was churning in her. His matter-of-fact tone grated on her nerves, and she realized that her hands were fisted and that her breathing was ragged.

"Or in my family," Brady said. "But to my knowledge, no one in my family ever married under such circumstances as we're facing."

"Couldn't it be that we're creating a tempest in a teapot?" Finley asked in a last-ditch effort to rid him of his foolish proposition. "Now think about it. Will anyone really *care* about our private lives?"

"I can think of two people—your dad and Kristi."

"Kristi!" The name sent a new wave of desolation through Finley and she slumped in defeat. "She's the culprit in this whole thing!"

"Yes and she's not easily put off, either," Brady reminded Finley. "She won't give up until she's made us miserable, and she'll destroy the team in the process."

Finley examined the lines on his forehead and realized that he was more upset than he sounded. She touched his hand and asked softly, "This whole thing really bothers you, doesn't it? Could it really blow a hole in your career?"

"Easily," he said after a pause. "We're sitting on a tinderbox, Finley. The team needs to have one thing in mind and that's winning the championship and not quibbling over people playing favorites. Understand?"

"Yes. I'm beginning to see your point."

"It could hurt your career, too, Finley," Brady said, squeezing her hand. "This is a fine opportunity for you, but this gossip will precede you when you work for other teams. Coaches and owners don't like to hire photographers who might stir up jealousy or turn their players' minds from football to romance during the season."

Finley sighed and chewed on her bottom lip for a few seconds. Brady's explanation and prophecies were beginning to make sense, and she didn't like the pictures that were forming in her mind. Desperation seized her and she pulled her hand from Brady's and stood.

"This just isn't fair! Why should we bend to others' nasty tongues and do something crazy like get married? Let them talk! We'll stand our ground and they'll finally shut up."

Brady leaned back against the couch, his arms stretched across the back of it. He fixed her with a cold look. "Yes, they'll eventually shut up, but it will take a while and I'm not in the frame of mind right now to take it. *I want that championship!* I've worked hard for it and I need the team behind me—with me—right now. Finley, please marry me. Please?"

The pleading note in his voice twisted her heart, and she slumped in defeat. She turned her back to him and stared at the unlit fireplace. She felt empty and cold. She swallowed once, then again, before she trusted herself to speak. When she did, it was just a whisper.

"I'll marry you, Brady. You win."

She heard him ease himself from the couch and move to stand behind her. He slipped his arms around her waist and pulled her against him. His lips touched her hair.

"Thanks, Red. It won't be so bad. You and I can pursue our careers and nobody's going to say anything about this past night to us. We'll be married and everyone will be happy for us."

Finley sighed and shut her eyes. "Yes. At least to our faces."

The initial public curiosity and excitement over the news that Finley Malone had married Bryan Brady was wearing off. The telephone had stopped ringing and people had stopped coming to the house to view the happy couple and offer sound advice and gushy exclamations.

Finley stretched in the bed and placed her hand to her forehead. The skin was cool and she decided that her cold was finally leaving her. For two weeks it had hung onto her, making her feverish and aching. She had decided that she had caught the cold in New York and the whirlwind trip to Las Vegas had just added fuel to the spark of illness.

Las Vegas. Finley wrinkled her nose when her mind flashed visions of the hasty wedding ceremony. Jilly, Gena, and her father had attended, and she was thankful for their support. She had been surprised when Bryan had agreed to let Jilly and Gena into the small group "in the know." Maybe he felt he would need one confidant, besides Mike Malone, Finley thought. She knew that it was a comfort already to be able to talk frankly with Gena. She would have probably gone crazy these past two weeks if it hadn't been for Gena's company and assurance that everything was going to work out and that Finley had done the right thing in marrying Bryan.

Finley recalled her father's unusual behavior at the wedding. He seemed elated. Finley had thought he would be sad and slightly disapproving that his only child was marrying a man not for love, but for necessity. After the ceremony, Mike Malone had embraced Finley and given her a wink of approval.

"I'll tell you a secret, Finley," he had whispered close to her ear. "I'm thinking of tying the knot, too!"

Finley had stared at him in shocked silence, then had smiled her approval.

"Yes," Mike said with a swift nod. "I'm thinking of asking Alicia to marry me. I'll be keeping close watch on you and Bryan to see how things work out."

Finley felt her smile fading. "I'm so happy for you, Dad, but don't look to us for a good example. We're hardly the loving couple."

"Oh, I think things will work out well for both of you, Finley, my girl. Bryan's a good man."

Finley had found herself speechless again. She kissed her dad's cheek and decided that weddings just had an odd effect on him. He had become wrapped up in the sentiment and in the lovely vows and had forgotten that the two people who repeated those vows were bound and determined to break them within a year.

Pulling her mind away from the past, Finley yawned and flipped the sheets and coverlet from her legs and climbed out of bed. A light tap sounded at the bedroom door, and Finley reached for her pale green dressing gown and slipped into it before answering the knock.

Martha, the housekeeper Bryan had hired to help Finley with the domestic chores, bustled into the bedroom. Her black, coarse hair was piled haphazardly into an untidy bun on the top of her round head and her jet-black eyes sparkled as she wished Finley a good morning.

Finley sat at the dressing table and brushed her hair while Martha made up the bed. She watched the woman's quick, sharp movements and thought that Martha was just the right type of housekeeper for an odd couple who were supposed to be newlyweds but who slept in separate bedrooms. When Finley had objected to a housekeeper, Bryan had held up a quieting hand.

"This woman won't be a gossip," he had told Finley. "When I started to explain our—situation, she told me that it wasn't any of her business and that she would rather not be told of personal matters. She's just what we need, Red."

Now, Finley caught Martha's stern profile in the mirror and smiled. Martha wasn't a big talker, but Finley knew that those coal-black eyes didn't miss much, if anything.

"Have you lived in Oklahoma all your life, Martha?"

Martha seemed surprised at the question, but she answered, with some pride, "Yes, missus."

Finley frowned at the label. She hated being called "missus" but Martha was determined to call her that. At first Martha had called her "Mrs. Brady," but when Finley informed her that she had kept her maiden name, the woman had scowled and started calling her "missus." She called Bryan "mister," but Bryan said he didn't mind. He said he'd been called much worse things.

Martha cleared her throat, then wiped a hand across her wrinkled brow. "My people came here during the Land Run."

"A true Sooner, are you?"

Martha nodded and almost smiled, but she seemed to catch herself in time. "You feeling good this morning, missus?"

Finley nodded. "Much, much better. I think I've whipped this cold. I don't have a fever today and I slept well last night."

"That's good." Martha straightened and surveyed the bed. She smoothed one wrinkle from the peach-colored bedspread, then rested her large, square hands on her hips. "You want breakfast?"

"Just coffee and toast, please. I suppose Brad—Bryan is at the gym today."

"Yes, he left early and said he wouldn't be here for dinner. Said he'd call later." Martha moved toward the door and her mouth curved in a frown. "He don't ever eat breakfast, either."

"He probably grabs something on the way to work, Martha."

"Humph!"

The sound was scornful, and Finley stopped brushing her hair and looked at Martha. The woman's expression was closed and guarded and she nodded and left the room. Finley let the brush clatter to the top of the table.

What does she expect me to do? Finley wondered. Tell Bryan that he'd better start eating a nutritious breakfast or I'll tell his mother on him?

His mother!

Finley gripped the edge of the dressing table and stared at her white, frightened face in the mirror. I haven't met his family, but I will! Bryan had persuaded them not to visit until after the Super Bowl—that is, if the team made the Super Bowl. Bryan refused to even *think* that the Wildcatters wouldn't be in the Super Bowl. Now they were tied for the conference lead with Dallas, and each game from here on was a "must win."

His family would meet them at the Super Bowl and Finley would be introduced to the large Brady clan—Mom, Dad, and the three sisters and four brothers, plus various in-laws. She shivered at the thought. What would she say to them?

Oh, hello. I imagine you're wondering why your son married me right out of the blue. Well, don't fret and don't worry about trying to get to know me, because I won't be around much longer. Your son's going to divorce me very soon. So nice to meet you. What? You don't want your son to divorce me? Well, you see, it's all been arranged . . .

Finley buried her face in her hands, blocking out the image and the hurtful words. The present situation was wearing on her. She knew that her cold had been a handy excuse for living like a hermit, and she knew that Bryan was aware of it too.

She recalled a few evenings ago when she had asked Bryan if his teammates had stopped prodding him about his marriage.

A lazy smile had found his lips and he had looked at her

with hooded eyes. "Yes. It's not so bad, you know. There hasn't been much of a discussion about my marriage to you. People get married every day. You'll find that out once you get over your cold—that is, if it doesn't develop into pneumonia or leprosy or some other contagious disease."

"What does that mean, Brady?" she had asked sharply.

"It *means* that you're going to have to face the music sooner or later and that it might as well be sooner because it's no big deal! *And* will you please start calling me by my *first* name?!" He had stood then and stormed upstairs. The bedroom door had slammed with such force that something had fallen from the wall to the floor and crashed. Finley had tensed and then, without knowing why, burst into tears. From that point on, however, she had made a concerted effort to call him by his Christian name.

Now, she removed her hands from her face and realized that, again, she was crying for no reason at all. Angry with herself, she grabbed a tissue and wiped the tears from her face. He's right, she thought. I have to face the music. I can't stay cooped up here forever and just see my Dad and Jilly and Gena. I have a career and it's waiting for me.

She stood and went to the closet to select a purple-and-violet colored caftan. She took a quick shower, then dressed in the caftan and added a touch of blush to her cheeks and pink coloring to her lips. The caftan had a gathered waist and a deep V-neck that revealed the tops of her creamy breasts. She shrugged and smiled at her reflection. Who are you dressing up for? she asked herself. Martha? Yourself? She scolded herself and went downstairs to the kitchen. Martha poured a cup of coffee and set it on the table along with a dish of toast.

Lost in thought, Finley buttered the toast and began to eat. Realizing that she was tasting nothing, she pushed the remaining toast away and sipped her coffee. She thought of Bryan and his coolness toward her since the wedding. Yes, he was preoccupied with his career right now, but there was something else drawing him from her. He seemed uncomfortable in her company and he went to every extreme to avoid being alone with her. He spent hours at the gym and at practice. Her dad had said that Bryan was obsessed with building himself up physically and making sure he would be at his peak on Super Bowl Sunday.

When they had returned from Las Vegas, Bryan had helped her move her things to his house and had talked the apartment owner into releasing her from her lease. But since her arrival in the house, he had barely spoken to her. He made it a habit to rise early and come home late. He seemed eager to leave town for games in other cities and seemed unhappy to return to his home. He seldom laughed or teased as he used to. Nowadays he was withdrawn and brooding, and when she spoke to him, he usually jumped and answered her with one-syllable words before he made a hasty retreat to his study or his bedroom.

His attitude infuriated Finley, and more than once, she had fought an urge to strike him or scream at him.

With a start, she realized that it was Sunday and there was a home game scheduled this afternoon. She glanced at her watch and saw that it was ten o'clock. Quickly, she left the kitchen and went to the telephone alcove in the hallway. She phoned Frank and waited impatiently as the telephone rang five times before Frank finally answered.

"Frank, I'm going to work the game today."

"Finley! Are you sure? How you feeling? Bryan says—"

"I'm fine now. I'll be there by one. The game starts at two o'clock, right?"

"Right. Are you sure—?"

"Positive. See you." Finley replaced the receiver and felt better than she had since that awful Las Vegas trip. What she needed was work, she told herself. She'd go mad if she kept moping around and thinking about Bryan and his ice-man attitude!

With a light step, she climbed the stairs and pulled a pair

of jeans, a gold cable-knit sweater, and boots and socks from her closet to wear that afternoon. It was cold outside, but the sun was shining. She hummed as she checked over her camera equipment and enjoyed the feeling of anticipation that grew inside of her.

For the first time in weeks, Finley felt as if she belonged to a real, warm, exciting world again. She stood in the tunnel outside the team dressing room and listened to the hoots and hollering of the players inside. Finley grinned at the sound of their noisy celebration.

The thrill of the game and her part in it still drugged her mind, lifting her to a dizzy height. She recalled the way her mind seemed to slip into high gear as she began taking pictures of the game. The Wildcatters had soundly whipped the Kansas City team and she had recorded the victory! The players had been shy and awkward around her at first, but by the end of the game they were teasing her and hugging her, making her feel like one of the team again. All the players, except one.

Bryan had ignored her after his first reaction of surprise at seeing her on the sidelines. For a moment, he had started toward her as if to say something to her, but then his face had hardened and he had spun away from her and joined her dad. Humiliation had pressed down on her, but the excitement of her craft had swept away the crushing feeling and left her breathless and feeling like a vibrant, alive woman.

Now, listening to the joy on the other side of the door, Finley leaned against the rough, cold wall and waited for Bryan. She wanted to go to the party being held at her father's home, and she wanted Bryan to escort her to that party.

Players were leaving the dressing rooms now and each one greeted her and asked if she was going to the party. She nodded her head, feeling her smile grow with each warm response of "Great! See you there! Glad you're back with us, Finley!"

Restless, she spied the water fountain and moved down the tunnel to take a cool drink of water. As she was bending over the fountain, someone passed her heading for the dressing room and she heard Kristi Sinclair's clear, confident voice.

"Hey, Bryan! I'm here and ready to party! You going to give me a lift?"

Finley straightened slowly and felt her face grow hot with blazing fury. She watched as Bryan smiled and placed a hand on Kristi's shoulder before his gaze lifted above the blonde's head to find Finley's own level glare. His smile faded and his mouth thinned in a tight-lipped frown. Kristi turned and her eyes widened, then narrowed quickly, when she spotted Finley.

"What are you doing here?" Kristi's question was blunt and insulting.

"Waiting for my husband." Finley heard her own tone and was surprised at the low, icy quality of it. "We're going to my father's party—I think."

"You feel well enough to go to a party?" Bryan asked, still not taking his eyes from her.

"I feel fine." Finley said each word slowly so there'd be no room for doubts or further questions.

Kristi tugged at the hem of her snug-fitting red sweater, pulling it just past the waistband of her tight blue jeans. She seemed to be waiting for Bryan to make a choice.

"Do you need a lift, Kristi? We'll take you." Bryan glanced at Kristi, then looked at Finley again, his eyes challenging her.

"Well..." Kristi glanced at him, then at Finley. "If it's not too much trouble."

Finley almost choked on her anger. She gripped her car keys, then tossed them to Bryan. He caught them and gave her a questioning look.

"Take the car. I'll catch a ride with someone else." Finley turned and walked quickly down the tunnel toward the fading sunlight.

"Finley!"

Bryan's angry voice echoed in the tunnel, but Finley didn't stop. She started running and stumbled into Jilly just outside the tunnel.

"Hey, little lady!" Jilly caught her shoulders and grinned at her. "Where's the fire?"

Finley sucked in some air, her lungs struggling for oxygen. "Jilly! Can you drop me by my house so that I can change for the party? Would it be too much trouble?"

Jilly looked over her head into the dark tunnel, and his face showed concern and confusion. "I— Sure, Finley. Need a ride to the party too? Gena and I can pick you up on the way."

"Oh, yes! Thanks!" Finley tucked her hand in the crook of his arm and almost dragged him to the car. Gena, in the front seat, looked startled to see her.

"We're going to give Finley a ride home to change for the party, then take her with us, honey," Jilly told his wife quietly.

"Oh." Gena turned in her seat to smile as Finley climbed into the back seat. "Great! I'm glad you're going to go, Finley. I'll have more fun with you there." Gena's expression clouded as she looked past Finley and out the back window of the car.

Finley turned to see Bryan and Kristi walking toward Bryan's sports car. She stiffened and turned back to face Gena. "I won't ride with her," she said with a cold edge to her voice.

Gena nodded. "Can't say I blame you. What's Bryan doing running around with her anyway after what she did?"

Finley shrugged. "Guess he's forgiven her."

Jilly shook his head. "Hasn't acted like it until now. He's been pretty cool around Kristi lately."

"Well, he's warmed up!" Finley bit her lip as her ears picked up the bitterness in her voice. She looked down at her clasped hands and felt tears smart her eyes. She vowed to herself that this party wouldn't be like the last one, when she'd left feeling lost and alone. No. She looked at the gold band on her third finger. I'm going to exercise my rights tonight, she thought. He'll not humiliate me any further—and Kristi Sinclair had better stay out of my way!

9

Mike Malone's house was alive with celebration. Lights and movement were evident from the outside of the house. Once inside, guests were greeted by decorations of gold and green and plenty of food and drinks. Mike was beaming and Alicia practically glowed as she stood by his side and greeted each newcomer. Alicia's smile grew when she saw Finley. She embraced Finley in a warm hug.

"Mike! Look who's up and about and looking stunning!" Alicia held Finley at arm's length, and her gaze traveled from Finley's curly russet hair, to her shining green eyes, to the silk shirt that matched the color of her hair, and finally to the black velour trousers. "Finley, you look like a high-fashion model!"

Finley laughed and tipped her head to receive her father's kiss on her cheek. "Just what I needed to balloon my ego, Alicia! Thank you."

"No thanks necessary," Mike told her with a grave look. "The lady is just stating a fact. You are lovely, honey." He gave her a smile that was both proud and full of foolish sentiment.

His smile made Finley's heart expand with love, and she kissed his ruddy cheek. "I love you, Dad. You're a sentimental old Irish fool. Did you know that?"

He grinned and patted her hand that rested on his arm. "Yes. Especially about you."

Finley let the good feelings rest in her heart for a few more precious moments before she addressed a less heart-warming subject. "Where's Bryan?"

Immediately the mood darkened and her father's warm expression faded. He nodded toward the bar. "Last time I saw him he was over there—with Kristi."

Finley nodded, then forced a smile to her lips. "Excuse me?"

"Have fun tonight, Finley," Alicia told her, placing a comforting hand on her shoulder. "You're young and you deserve this evening to lighten your spirits and make you see the world through rose-colored glasses again."

Finley studied the woman's kind, lovely face for a moment and decided that she wouldn't mind having Alicia as a stepmother. She smiled gratefully, then left Mike and Alicia to find her husband.

Finley spotted Bryan across the room. He was standing with several players near the glass doors that opened to the patio. Dressed in a gray suit and a heather-colored turtlenecked sweater, he seemed boldly Irish. His hair was a bit tousled, the blond and light red strands catching the light, and his striking blue eyes were focused on Jilly's animated face. He held a glass in one hand, and Finley guessed that the glass held a measure of brandy. Suddenly, his eyes sparkled at something Jilly said and his lips twitched into that familiar lopsided grin.

Finley's heart fluttered like a wild thing as she watched him. Tearing her gaze away from his compelling presence, she forced herself to survey the room. She found Kristi lounging near the bar, surrounded by men. Satisfied, Finley looked back to Bryan and found him staring at her.

His expression told her nothing. His dark blue gaze roamed her figure, hesitating momentarily on the swell of her breasts beneath the silky, clinging shirt, before raking her face again. He murmured something to his companions, then walked toward her, his stride graceful and unhurried.

Finley felt as if she were glued to the spot. A part of her wanted to run as he approached her, but her heart hammered out a message to stay put and confront him.

He stopped just in front of her. "Is that outfit new?"

Surprised at his question, she stammered, "Wh-what? Oh, no. No-no. It's not—new."

A shadow of a smile passed over his face. "It's nice. Would you like a drink or something to eat?"

She started to say yes, then remembered that Kristi stood near the bar. "No, thanks. I'd like to dance."

One eyebrow lifted slightly, then he placed his drink on a tray that was being whisked past him by a waiter. He held out his hands to her. "Then, by all means, let's dance."

Joy threatened to intoxicate her as she moved into the circle of his arms and began to match the tempo of his lead. He held her gently, slightly away from him so that he could look down into her upturned face. Magic seemed only a heartbeat away, and Finley wanted to reach out and capture it and hold it close.

"You made a fool of yourself earlier this evening, Finley."

His whispered statement shattered the magic moment. Finley drew away from him, but his arm tightened about her waist to keep her prisoner. She swallowed the pain and disappointment that was lodged in her throat.

"That is debatable, and I refuse to argue the point this evening," Finley said, her voice calm.

"Another thing to be swept under the rug, is that it?"

She frowned, angry at him for spoiling her good mood. "No, that is not it. I'm here to enjoy myself, not to argue with you."

The music stopped and Mike Malone moved to the center of the large living room and held up his hands. Brady released Finley and faced the coach.

"Now that I have you all here . . ." Mike paused for the room to become silent. "I have an announcement." He turned to Alicia and grasped her hand. "I'm adding another person to our family. Alicia and I are going to be married right after the Super Bowl, so you guys had better win because that's what I want as a wedding present."

Shouts and applause sounded in the room, and Finley sucked in her breath and looked at Alicia. The woman's face glowed with happiness and she looked at Mike and lifted her lips for his kiss. Finley smiled, noticing the loving expression on her father's face as he kissed Alicia. It's right, she thought. Right as rain.

"How's that grab you, Red?"

Finley turned to Bryan, the smile still on her lips. "I'm happy for both of them. They love each other."

He seemed surprised at her reaction. "You mean that, don't you?"

"Of course! Dad deserves to have a woman who loves and needs him. He's been alone too long."

"He's had you."

Finley shook her head. "It's not the same thing. He needed a passionate love, not just a companion."

"Don't we all."

Finley blinked, then recoiled from the biting edge in Bryan's voice and words. His meaning was all too clear, and she didn't know how to address it, or if she should try.

Bryan laughed in the face of her dilemma. "Come on, let's get something to eat." He placed a hand on her elbow and guided her toward the buffet table.

Finley's throat constricted and her heart beat dully, painfully, as she approached the buffet table and Kristi Sinclair. Kristi moved to one side to allow them to fill their plates, and she gave Finley a secret, smirking smile.

"Sounds like you're going to get a stepmother," Kristi said.

"Sounds like it," Finley replied, busying herself with selecting thin slices of roast beef, carrot sticks, deviled eggs, and potato salad.

"I guess you're feeling better. You—you acted like you were ill earlier today," Kristi said, her voice taunting.

"I wasn't ill earlier today, Kristi, just disgusted at seeing you," Finley told her evenly.

"What?" Kristi looked as if she'd been slapped.

"You heard me." Now Finley turned to look directly at the other woman. "Bryan may have forgiven you for the spiteful, childish way you spread gossip about our private affairs, but I have not and never will. Excuse me." Finley pushed past her, ignoring the woman's open-mouthed surprise and not daring to look at Bryan's face. She picked up a fork and napkin and moved toward the patio, knowing that Bryan was right behind her.

"Do you enjoy making scenes, Finley? Do you enjoy airing your dirty laundry in front of everybody?"

Bryan's voice was angry, and Finley sat on one of the redwood benches and set her plate in her lap. She looked up at him and examined his flushed face and the veins that protruded in his strong neck. He was furious.

"She had that coming and she was baiting me," Finley told him, then took a nibble at a carrot stick.

"*Who* behaved childishly in there, Finley?! Look at me!"

Finley obeyed him and resisted the urge to cringe from the dark glitter in his eyes.

He balled his hands into fists. "Why did you come tonight? To stir up trouble?"

"It seems to me that Kristi is the one who's doing the stirring," Finley said.

A muscle jerked in Bryan's jaw. "For two weeks I've endured countless questions about why we married and why we didn't tell anyone prior to our hasty decision. Things finally settled down to normal and the guys forgot the whole thing and started talking about winning instead of about my private life and now!" He rocked on the balls of his feet as if he was preparing to pounce on her. "Now, you start this catfighting. Why don't you ignore her? Why do you have to bite at her bait?"

"Because I'm tired of taking all the dishing out!" Finley

whispered fiercely, then glanced around to make sure they were alone. "How dare you take her to the party! How *dare* you be seen with her! Have you forgotten that she's the reason for all this—this mess we're in?"

"And I'll take care of her—privately. I've already talked to her about this. What I don't want is people taking sides."

"Taking sides?" Finley shook her head in confusion.

"Yes. If we start quarreling with Kristi in public, then our friends will feel compelled to take our side or Kristi's. I don't want that to happen, so you let me handle it and keep that Irish temper of yours under control!"

Reason replaced rage in Finley's mind and she began to bend toward Bryan's logic. She tipped her head to one side and asked, "Just what have you told Kristi about us?"

Bryan sat beside her and lifted a carrot stick from her plate. He bit into the carrot and chewed for a moment. "I've just explained to her that I didn't tell anybody about marrying you because I wanted to surprise everybody after the New York game."

"And she believes that?"

He shrugged. "No, but that's not my problem—or yours."

"I still think it was rude and spiteful of you to offer to give her a ride to the party," Finley said, then hurried on before he could speak. "I won't change my mind about that, so save your breath. Are you taking her home, too?"

Bryan swallowed the morsel of carrot and sighed. "I don't know."

Finley placed her plate in his lap and stood. She glared down at him. "Well, let me know, because if you do take her home, I won't be riding with you."

"What's with you?" Bryan demanded.

"I am not going to those extremes of being nice to her, that's all. You make your choice. Either you take her home or me—and if you take her home, then don't bother coming back to the house, stay with her!" Finley was stunned by her own, hateful words, but she refused to take any of them back. She stared at Bryan and watched his eyes grow dark and menacing.

"Is that so?" he asked as he studied her through narrowed lids. "Let me remind you that that house is *mine* and you can't keep me out of it."

"Then I'll find somewhere else to stay!" Anger mixed with embarrassment in Finley and served to fuel her mind and tongue with foolish words. "I won't live under the same roof with you if you continue to court and play around with Kristi Sinclair!"

He set the plate on the bench and stood to tower over her. His hands found her shoulders and his fingers dug into her skin. "Watch your tongue, Finley! Don't you start accusing me of things like that or I might exercise my rights as a husband and—and—"

"And what?" Finley asked, lifting her chin in a defiant gesture.

"And take what is mine!" He pulled her to him, none too gently, and his mouth crushed hers in an angry, fiery kiss.

Finley sucked in her breath in mute shock, and then a wave of passion washed over her. She clung to him and matched the intensity of his kiss, her lips parting under the pressure of his mouth. His hands moved from her shoulders to caress her back through the rich fabric of her blouse, and Finley mirrored his caresses with those of her own. Her hands moved up and down his broad back and she could feel the ripple of muscle as he moved to bind her closer to his embrace. His mouth left hers to plant kisses on her nose and cheeks and his breath was warm on her skin when he whispered to her in a rough, masculine tone.

"So this is what you've been wanting, is it? Why didn't you just say so and I would have obliged on our wedding night? You're not mad at Kristi; you're mad at me for not seeing how much you wanted to be with me."

Finley pushed him from her and added space between the passion she had felt a moment ago and the shocked horror

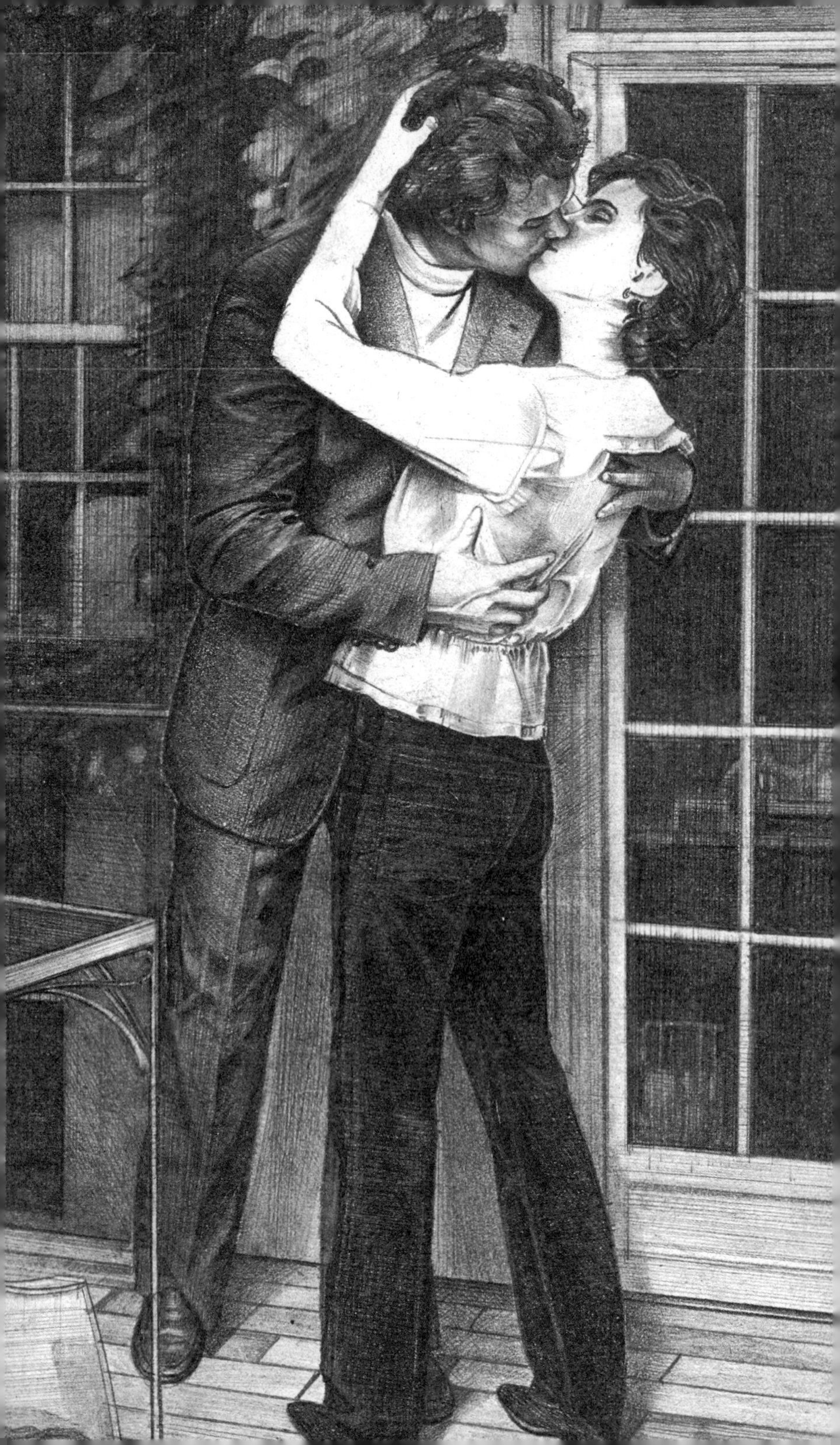

she was feeling now. She knew that her face had drained suddenly of color and that her flushed lips trembled as she looked at him. He took a step toward her, and she backed away, shaking her head.

"No! Don't you touch me! You—you conceited, disgusting—" Again, she shook her head as the words refused to form quickly enough. "Is that what you think? That I'm frustrated because you haven't paid attention to me? Let me dissuade you of that notion right way. I'm disgusted and frustrated because of this whole charade!"

"Keep your voice down!" he commanded through gritted teeth.

"Don't tell me what to do!"

"I'm taking you home," he announced, reaching for her hand.

Finley jerked from him. "No you are not! I won't let this spoil my father's party. I'm going back in there to have a good time, and I want you to keep your distance!" She spun from him and marched into the living room. Inside, she composed herself with some struggle, then moved toward her father and Alicia. They smiled at her and she smiled back, then tensed when she felt Bryan at her side.

"Having a good time?" her father asked.

"Wonderful," Finley answered, moving to his side, away from Bryan. "Congratulations, Dad. I'm so happy you're going to marry Alicia." She kissed her dad's cheek, then kissed Alicia.

"We wanted your blessing," Alicia told her. "Thank you." Alicia looked at Bryan. "Bryan, is something wrong?"

Bryan shook his head. "No. Congratulations, coach, I approve wholeheartedly."

Mike grinned and pumped Bryan's extended hand. "I have you and Finley to thank for bringing Alicia back into my life."

"Hey, Bryan!"

Bryan turned toward the sound of Jilly's voice. Jilly motioned for him to join a group of players on the other side of the room. Bryan turned back to Finley.

"I'm being summoned," he said. "Jilly and the others seem to want my expert advice. Excuse me, darling?"

Finley fumed at the pet name and forced a smile to her lips. "By all means. I can amuse myself quite well." She watched him join the other men, then sought out Gena. She needed a sympathetic ear desperately.

The house was quiet as Finley made her way downstairs. Hazy sunlight poured through the windows to play amid shadows on the carpet. Martha wouldn't be in today. She never worked on Mondays because Bryan wanted Mondays all to himself to recover from Sunday's game and post-game party. Mondays were quiet and the house seemed to vibrate with silence as Finley tiptoed to the kitchen.

A pot of coffee sat on a warmer and a cup and saucer on the table told her that Bryan was awake and somewhere in the house. It was too early to go to the gym. She looked into the cup and saw the wet residue there. She touched the cup and found it still warm. Her eyebrows rose in a questioning expression as she wondered where he could be. The basement, where his weights and a whirlpool tub waited to smooth out his knotted muscles and ease his post-game aches?

Bryan's muffled moan drifted up the basement stairs and into the kitchen, and Finley pressed a startled hand to her throat. She heard movement below and she moved quietly to the door that led to the basement. She stopped at the threshold and pulled her gold dressing gown closer to her body. He had been stony last night when they had arrived home. Once inside, he had retired to his bedroom and Finley to hers. She could hear him moving about all night through the connecting door and she knew he was walking off his fury. Still, she knew she was right. His callous, conceited remarks at the party demanded an apology, which he had refused to give, and she vowed she would not forgive him until he repented.

She felt herself weaken even as she repeated her vow to herself. He wasn't entirely wrong in his remarks, she admitted. She had examined her own motives last night while sleep eluded her and finally had come to the conclusion that she was falling in love with her husband. The thought was so ironic that Finley smiled. Falling in love with her husband. Yes. That accounted for the jealousy that loomed inside her when Kristi gave her that possessive sneer. Also, it accounted for her sweeping passion at the touch of his lips on hers. Passion that fired her and made her quiver with anticipation and longing.

A sound that was part groan and part sigh reached her, and she listened a moment longer, then tiptoed down the stairs. Bryan was lying on a metal table, a towel wrapped about his waist. He was lying on his stomach, facing away from her, and she was quiet as she walked toward him. She stopped a few feet from him, letting her gaze drink in his tanned skin, strong neck, heavy hair. Pools of water on the tile floor told her that he had been soaking in the whirlpool tub, and his body still glistened with tiny drops of water.

He shifted on the table, turning his head so that he faced her. Dark circles rested under his eyes as evidence to a sleepless night, and the sight twisted Finley's heart with unaccountable guilt. His mouth was slack and she found herself staring at a freckle on his lower lip. She smiled and felt something warm and wonderful curl inside her.

His lashes moved, then lifted to reveal sleepy blue eyes. He started when he saw her, rising slightly from the table, only to fall back upon it when he recognized his intruder. Finley stood rooted to the spot and waited to see if he would order her from his mini-gym or let her stay.

"Well, you could make yourself useful by giving me a massage, or you can stand there like a voyeur," he said finally, his voice gruff with sleep and exhaustion.

Finley hesitated only a moment before she moved to stand

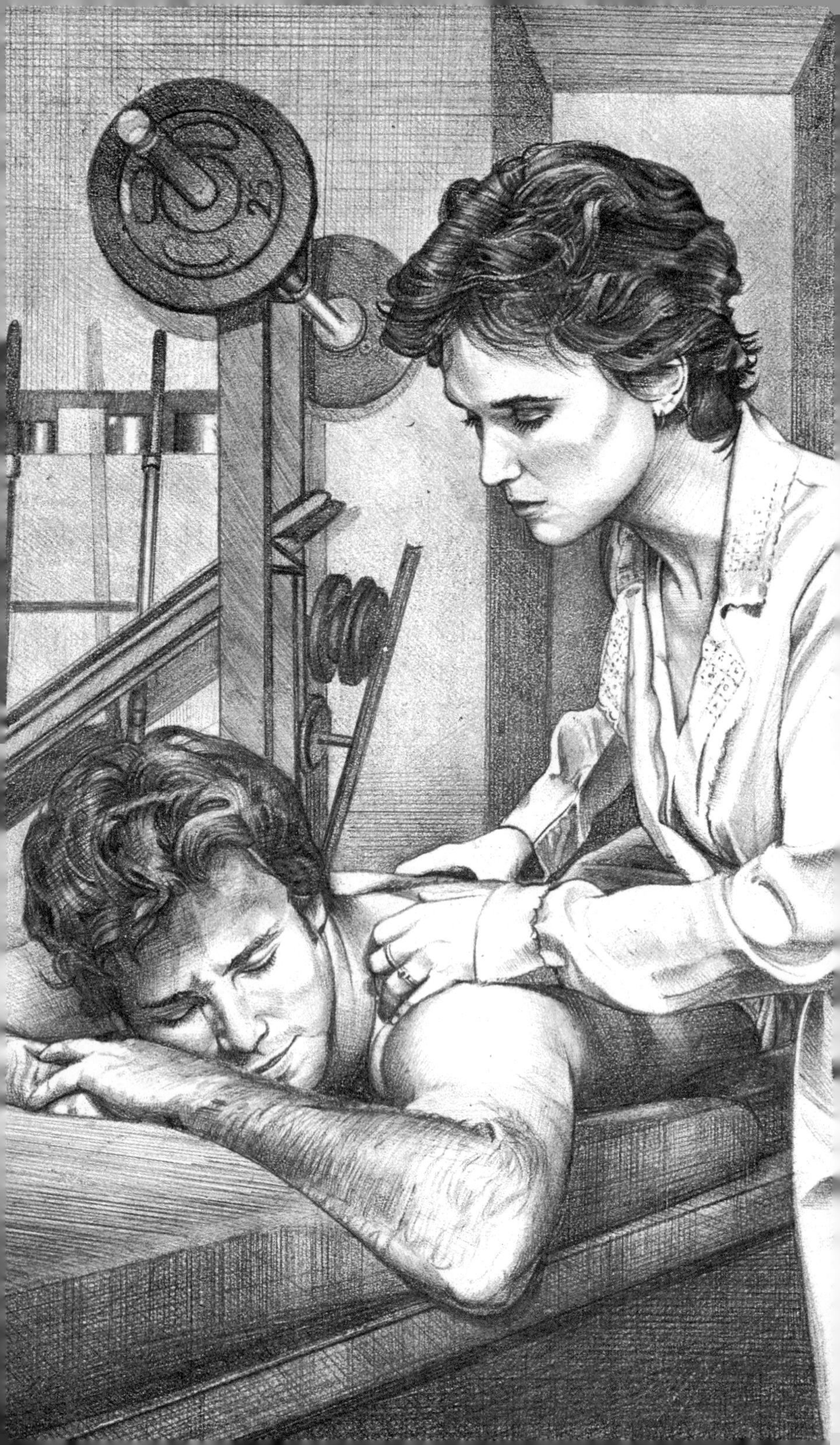

beside the table. She placed her hands lightly on his shoulders and felt the knotted muscles there. Knitting her eyebrows in concern, she began to knead the smooth flesh beneath her hands. His skin was warm and vibrantly masculine feeling, and she smiled as she massaged the bunched muscles. Gradually she felt him relax beneath her ministrations, and he closed his eyes with a contented sigh.

Her hands and fingers began to ache after half an hour, and she decided she would have to stop after she massaged his spine. Carefully, she pressed her fingers in tiny circles at the base of his spine and smiled when he groaned appreciably. She lifted her hands from him, then in a sudden spark of mischief, she slapped his backside.

"There! All done!"

"Not quite!"

He turned quickly onto his back and his strong hands circled her wrists and jerked her forward. Finley uttered a short shriek before she found herself lying on top of him and looking down into his handsome, teasing face. Again her gaze was arrested by the freckle on his full, lower lip and a tantalizing tingle raced up her spine when she saw him lift his head and touch his lips to hers. He didn't kiss her fully, but only brushed her lips slowly once, twice, three times with his own.

Finley smiled, enjoying his light progress and feeling that warmth curl tighter in her stomach, then spread its glow throughout her body. His hands found the small of her back and he pressed her closer to him, letting his lips travel lightly across her cheek until they found her mouth again. He kissed her, softly at first, then with a growing hunger that took her breath away. Her own hands rested on his shoulders and she stroked him and caressed him and found herself thinking over and over again, "I love you, Bryan . . . I love you. . . ."

Somehow she found herself in his arms and he was standing and moving toward the staircase that led to the kitchen. She wrapped her arms around his neck and rested her head on his shoulder. He climbed the stairs nimbly, his arms tightening around her, and strode through the house and up the other flight of stairs toward his bedroom. Finley looked around the familiar room, her gaze arrested by the large waterbed. She recalled the night she had slept beside him . . . the night that had led to a wedding and to this moment.

Her gaze searched for his and found it. In the depths of his eyes she saw a moment of hesitation, as if he were giving her a chance to draw away from him, but she could not. Her heart fluttering, she dipped her head in a slight nod, her lips touching his collarbone. Her gaze caught sight of a pulse beating quickly in his neck and her ears caught the sound of a gasp of pleasure as he moved toward the bed. Gently, he placed her there, then came to lie beside her. Mild surprise filtered through her when she realized that he had shed the towel and was now untying the sash of her dressing gown with hands that trembled slightly. His eyes drank in the creamy texture of her skin and his fingers found the hard peaks of her breasts and skimmed them until she quivered with longing.

Hungry lips touched hers, then slid over her mouth possessively. Finley opened her mouth to his seeking and a soft moan filtered up from her chest as his tongue curled around her own. Finley grasped his shoulders as he shifted position to cover her body with his own.

The firm pressure of his body sent a shiver snaking the length of her spine and she arched to gather him closer, loving the feel and play of the muscles that rippled and writhed beneath his skin. He whispered her name, the sound echoing in her head until her name became a lover's chant. His mouth moved to capture hers then continued down the side of her neck as his hands explored the pleasure points of her waist and stomach. Finley smoothed her hands down his back to rest on his hips in a tight embrace.

"I want you so much, Finley."

His voice was hoarse and his breath hot upon her skin.

Finley swallowed her pounding pulse and wet her lips with the tip of her tongue as her fingers dug into the flesh of his hips.

"Then make me yours, Bryan . . . Bryan . . ." The words died in her throat as he moved slowly, deliberately to obey.

Warm sunlight bathed Finley, and she turned her head to fill her eyes with Bryan.

He slept beside her, one strong arm tucked around her waist. She smiled and felt the love for him well within her and threaten to overflow in silly, sentimental tears. She batted her lashes and swallowed the lump of emotion.

Bryan stirred and opened his eyes. He gave her a lazy smile and pulled her closer. His lips found hers in a soft, warm kiss that told her more than words of endearment.

"Ummmmm," he moaned with a little growl. "This is the best Monday I've ever had."

"Just the best Monday?" Finley asked with a smile.

He grinned. "The best day, period." He kissed her bare shoulder, then nibbled lightly, laughing when she protested. "You're sweet enough to eat, Red."

"Well, control your urges, please."

Eyes as blue as the seven seas sparkled at her as his mouth formed a lopsided grin. "No can do, lady. I'm an animal." He growled again and laughed at her shriek. His mouth covered hers in a kiss that shattered her playful mood and left a passionate, craving woman in its wake.

"I love you, Bryan," she whispered, but he didn't seem to hear her. His mind was on other things as he bent to his pleasurable task.

10

Patches of melting snow dotted the grassy area around the circular pond and the majestic fountain was frozen in a breathtaking spew of cascading icicles.

"This has always been my favorite place," Finley told Bryan as they walked hand in hand along the chain-link fence that kept spectators away from the lake and the creatures that inhabited it. "Swan Lake. It's lovely, isn't it?"

Bryan nodded, squeezing her hand. "Did you ever neck here?"

"What?" Finley turned her head to see his mischievous expression. "Certainly not!"

"I'll bet!" He laughed and stopped to lean against the fence and watch some ducks waddle near the shore.

Finley joined him and giggled as the ducks began roughhousing and splashing in the cold, clear water. She savored the sunny afternoon and decided she had never been so happy. For the first time she felt like a wife, like a woman who was loved and cherished by a special man. If I were a cat, she thought, I'd be purring right now.

A smile crossed her lips at the thought and she crossed her arms along the top of the fence and let her gaze roam over the chilly lake. Two swans were gliding gracefully near the stone fountain, their necks arched and their black-masked faces looking serene. Game ducks wiggled their feathered tails and squawked as they chased each other. Finley lifted her gaze to examine the houses that ringed the area. How I'd love to live here, she thought. To be so near to such beauty must be wonderful. To have this scene part of your daily life would be so peaceful and secure.

"The houses along here are beautiful, aren't they?" Bryan asked, as if reading her thoughts. "Wouldn't mind living here, would you?"

"I was just thinking how perfect it would be," Finley admitted. "You don't often see For Sale signs in the yards here, though."

"Yes, well, that makes sense. Who'd want to move?" He pushed himself from the fence and draped an arm about Finley's shoulders. "Let's walk."

"This place is really unique," Finley observed as she walked beside Bryan. "It's a haven, here in the heart of Tulsa, surrounded by concrete and tall buildings."

"Tulsa's miniature version of New York's Central Park," Bryan said with a smile. "A spot of peace in a whirling city."

"I'm so happy, Bryan." Finley colored at her bold statement and at Bryan's surprised expression.

"Are you?" He hugged her closer to him and smiled. "So am I, Finley. So am I." He kissed the top of her head and guided her toward the car.

"Are we leaving?" Finley asked, not bothering to hide the disappointment she felt.

Bryan laughed and opened the car door. "Let's go to another park."

"Which one?" Finley eased into the passenger side and Bryan closed the door. She watched him round the front of the sportscar and then sit beside her.

"Riverparks. Ever been to the Western village there?"

"No! Where is it?"

Bryan smiled, glanced over his shoulder to check for approaching automobiles, then steered the car from its parking place and onto the main street. "On the west bank. It's a miniature village for kids."

"Oh." Finley turned to look at him. "I don't think I've even been on the west bank of the river."

"You really know your own city, don't you?" he teased.

Finley shrugged. "I'm guilty. I guess the human tendency is to explore everyplace but your own backyard. Did you know Boston well?"

He shook his head. "Not as well as most visitors. You'll have to go there sometime with me and I'll show off my hometown."

A thrill feathered through her and she cast a sidelong glance at Bryan. He's talking as if we'll be together for some time, she thought, and a wave of hope washed through her.

Oh, my, when did I fall so desperately in love with this man? she wondered. How ironic that I've fallen in love with the man I swore I'd hate.

Her predicament sent a smile to her lips and she turned in her seat to examine the man who had come to mean so much to her. The wind had ruffled his hair, letting it fall onto his wide forehead. Finley suppressed an urge to run her fingers through the red and blond strands, smoothing it from his forehead and feeling the rich texture of it. His eyes were hooded, shading themselves from the sun, and his lashes were long and dark, drawing more attention to the incredibly blue eyes. His hands, resting on the steering wheel, were large and strong, and Finley smiled when her gaze rested on his gold wedding band.

My husband.

The words sent a quiver of passion and pride through her and she gripped her hands in her lap to keep from embracing him and holding him to her trembling body. She turned her thoughts to the little, important things she liked about him. His deep, rich voice. That teasing glint in his eyes. The way his hands seemed to know her. That disarming lopsided smile that had melted her even when she had tried to hate him.

Do you know how you affect me? she asked him silently.

Do you know how much I want this—this strange marriage to work?

He glanced at her and she lowered her lashes and felt her skin grow hot. When she lifted her lashes she saw him smile knowingly, and a prickly warmth surfaced to her skin. He opened his mouth, as if to say something, then seemed to decide against it and Finley felt disappointment color her mood. What had he been going to say? The possibilities were numerous, but only one seemed to burn in her mind. That he loved her? Could that be it? Oh, why didn't he say it? Why? Those words would seal their unspoken commitment. Those words would chase away the nagging, troublesome thoughts she'd had since last night, when she had rested in his arms and glowed with an inner light.

He braked the car to a stop and killed the engine. "Here we are. We'll have to walk the rest of the way."

"I don't mind." Finley scrambled from the car, suddenly anxious to shatter the intimacy of the car's interior. She pulled on her gloves as a cold breeze touched her, reminding her of the winter weather despite the bright sun overhead.

Again his arm rested on her shoulders as he guided her along a path that snaked through the park. Since it was a weekday, few people were in the park. Finley smiled at a woman who was pushing a baby carriage and at the toddler who stumbled along beside her. Two young women jogged past, and Finley couldn't suppress the proud smile that captured her lips when the two women gave Bryan appreciative glances.

He did look particularly attractive in his jeans and brown suede coat. His boot heels clicked along the sidewalk and Finley had to hurry her steps to keep up with his long, easy stride.

He stopped and motioned ahead. "There it is. Makes you feel like a kid again, doesn't it?"

Finley gasped in delight at the child-sized western town. She walked ahead of Bryan to examine the jail, saloon, and hotel. A stagecoach stood before the town, and the area was sanded to create a huge, fun-filled sandbox.

"Oh!" Finley turned to face Bryan. "This is wonderful! I *do* feel like a kid."

"Really?" It was a slow drawl and his eyes sparkled. He ducked inside the jail and peered at her through the bars. "You'll never take me alive!"

She laughed at his evil expression. "Who are you? Black Bart?"

"Black Bart? Don't insult me! I'm the Mad Irishman, the meanest, orneriest gunman around these parts." He growled at her, showing his even, white teeth. "Who are you, little lady?"

Finley placed her hands on her hips and considered the question. "I'm Cattle Annie!" She pointed her finger at him, pistol style. "And you're a dead man, Mad Irishman."

He ducked from her view and Finley ran to the jail and looked in. He was gone. She stepped back and surveyed the other buildings. Nothing moved. Cautiously, she entered the saloon and felt the hair on the nape of her neck lift as she darted her gaze left and right in search of a moving figure. A delicious thrill of anticipation ran up her spine as she moved along the buildings. She had to stoop a little, since the structures were meant for smaller "children." She winced as her boots sounded loudly in the still air.

When she'd examined the last building and found no Mad Irishman there, she frowned and felt something akin to fear. Where *is* he?

She emerged from the hotel and looked around. A sudden movement caught her eye and she had to smother a shriek.

"Ah ha!" Bryan laughed, a sinister sound, as he stood atop the stagecoach and aimed his pistol-finger at her. "Say your prayers, Cattle Annie!"

Instinctively, she brought up her own weapon and fired an imaginary shot at him. His face crumpled and he grabbed his chest, then, almost in slow motion, he doubled over and fell to the sand-packed ground. He landed with a thump on his back and groaned, then he was still.

Finley laughed, then sobered when he failed to scramble to his feet. She crept forward. "Bryan? Bryan?" A worried frown found her face as she advanced toward him. "Bryan!" She leaned over him, examining his frozen grimace, then she touched his shoulder. "Bryan Brady, this isn't funny. You're scaring me."

His eyelashes moved, then lifted to reveal sparkling, blue eyes. His hands shot out to grab her shoulders and pull her off balance. Finley landed on top of him, and before she could utter a protest, his lips were on hers. Finley squirmed, but the sweet pleasure of his mouth took the fight from her and she melted in his arms. She willingly parted her lips and let her fingers comb through his hair. Finally, lifting her mouth from his, she gave him a scolding look.

"You're devious," she told him, fighting the smile that tugged at the corners of her mouth.

"One of my more charming qualities," he replied, his hands resting on her waist in a protective, easy embrace. "Kiss me."

Finley glanced up to see if any spectators were present, and Bryan raised his head from the sand and found her mouth in a lazy, exploring kiss. Finley's insides churned with burning passion and she wished for a more secluded location. Her arms went beneath his neck and she held him close, urging on his intense exploration of her mouth. Bryan pulled away, and his eyes were dark with passion.

"We'd better go," he said.

Finley looked down into his face, watching the play of conflicting emotions there. She smiled at his misery and scrambled to her feet. Her hands trembled as she brushed sand from her jeans and black leather coat. She clapped her hands together to dislodge the sand from her wool gloves and laughed as Bryan ruffled his hair to try to brush the sand out of it.

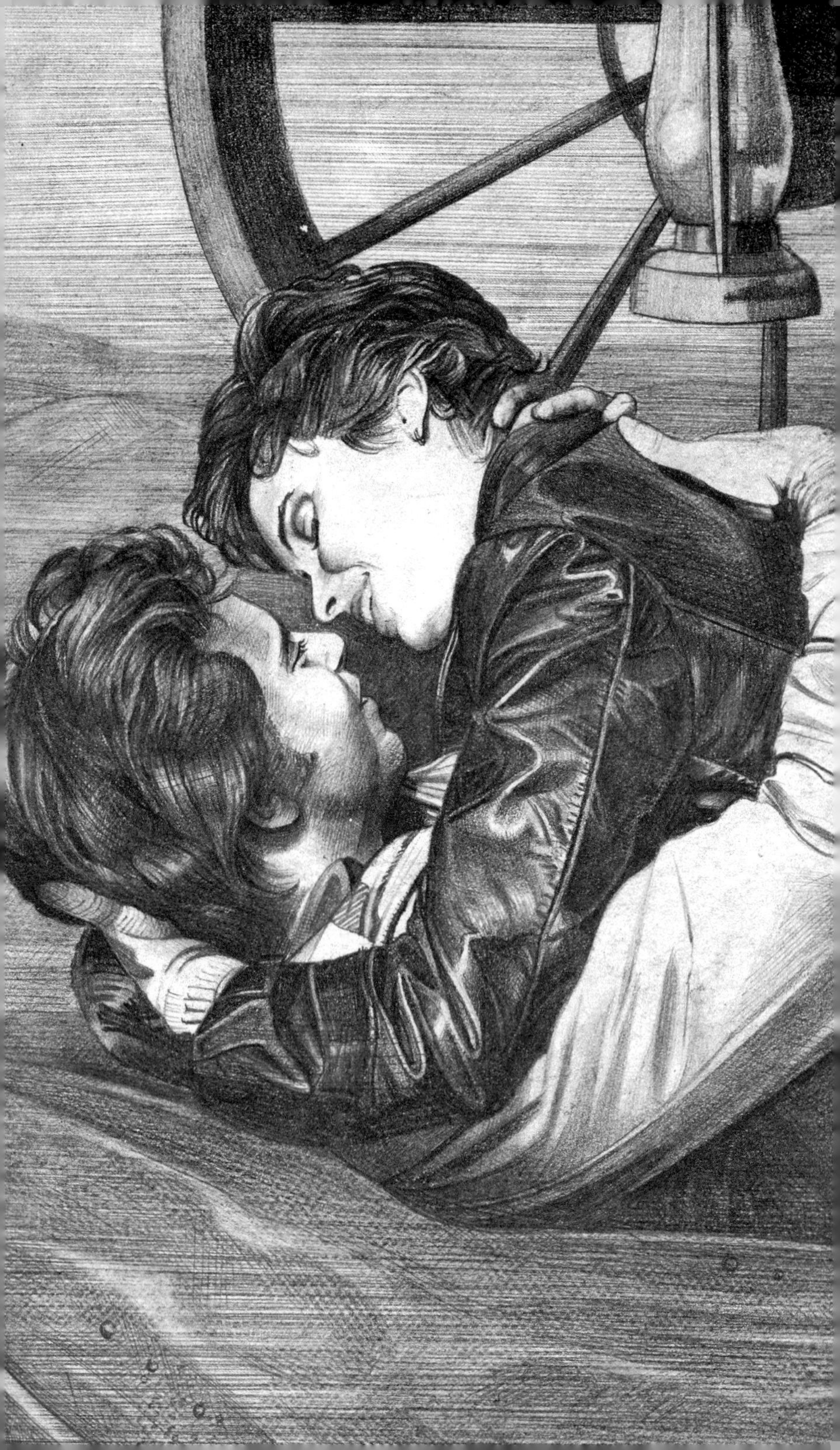

"What a gritty mess!" he grumbled.

"That's what you get for scaring me like that," Finley told him, still laughing.

He smiled and held out a hand to her. "Come on, Cattle Annie. Let's go get some lunch."

She took his hand, loving the feel of strength there, and began walking with him back to the car. She glanced over her shoulder at the western town and felt her heart swell with deep emotion. That will be a special place from now on, she thought, a place that will always make me think of us—no matter what the future holds.

Determined not to allow herself to think of the dark side of their relationship, Finley faced forward and concentrated on the present—the present that contained her and Bryan and a happiness that made her heart soar.

Bryan selected a tearoom in a nearby shopping mall for lunch. High-backed booths gave each group of customers a sense of privacy, and Finley enjoyed the atmosphere and the delicious lunch of tuna salad, bread sticks, dill pickles, cherry torte, and black coffee.

Relaxing over a cup of English breakfast tea and butter cookies, Finley saw Bryan glance across the room and lift a hand in greeting. She followed his gaze and saw a man in his forties smile at them. His companion was a lovely woman with black, wavy hair and large green eyes. When she lifted her hand in a short wave, Finley caught the sparkle of a diamond wedding band.

"Finley, would you excuse me for a few minutes?" Bryan asked. "That's an old friend of mine and I'd better go blue-sky with him or he'll feel slighted."

"Yes, of course."

"Thanks." He wiped the corners of his mouth with the linen napkin. "I'll just be a minute."

Finley watched him approach the couple, then she sipped her tea and let the happiness flow through her as she pondered her good luck. A lovely winter day, a good lunch, pleasing surroundings, and a man she loved with all her heart: what more could she ask for? She let a satisfied sigh slip through her lips.

Again she glanced across the room at him and thought what a striking man he was dressed in the tight blue jeans that hugged his muscled thighs and tapered hips. He'd shed his coat to reveal the jade green sweater over a white shirt. The brushed leather cowboy boots completed the outfit that seemed overwhelmingly masculine and rugged to Finley. Suddenly, she longed for him to finish his social deed and take her home. Home, where they could be alone and where she'd feel more at ease in touching him, caressing him, holding him . . .

"Have you gotten to know Bryan Brady's wife yet?"

Finley jumped and looked around her to find no one.

"No, and I'm not that worried about it."

Again, Finley jumped in her seat, but now she realized that the voices were coming from the booth behind her, the occupants hidden by the tall backs of the booths.

"Why not?"

Finley didn't recognize that voice, but the other woman was most assuredly Tanya Roberson, wife of one of the guards on the team. Finley wrinkled her nose. She'd never liked that woman or her husband. They were forever whispering behind people's backs and giggling. Gena called them the "I Know A Secret Twosome," but had admitted that whatever the Robersons were saying was too often more than gossip—it was really correct.

"I just—well . . ." Tanya paused dramatically and Finley could imagine the coy look that must be covering her face. "Let's just say that I'm not taking the trouble to get acquainted with Finley. She's just in on a pass."

Finley felt as if she'd been slapped. She blinked and tears collected in her wide eyes. She realized that her mouth was forming a shocked O and she snapped her jaws shut.

"In on a pass?" the other woman asked. "What do you mean by that?"

"I *mean* that she's not really a *wife*. Bryan just married her because—well, the coach staged a sort of shotgun wedding."

Finley closed her eyes and felt her stomach churn with misery. Shut up! Shut up! The words blared in her mind.

"A shotgun wedding? I can't believe it!"

"Believe it," Tanya said confidently. "He's still seeing Kristi. That wedding didn't stop him from playing around, oh, no! You know Bryan. He can't settle down with one woman, especially one that's forced on him. I'll bet that after the Super Bowl we won't see Finley around and— Oh! Hello, Bryan!"

Finley opened her eyes to see Bryan approaching. She wondered if he'd caught any of the conversation, but his happy expression told her he hadn't. He smiled, nodded toward the two women, and raised a hand in greeting.

"Hello, Tanya! Hi, Anne. Good to see you." He eased into the long seat, pressing himself close to Finley and resting an arm across her shoulders. He kissed her cheek, then narrowed his eyes. "Is something wrong, honey?"

"No. Please don't call me that." Finley couldn't speak above a whisper because suddenly her throat was dry and scratchy.

"What? Honey?" He sighed his irritation. "Believe me, I mean it with all due respect. I don't call just everybody—"

"I don't like it," she interrupted him. "I have a name."

He frowned at her. "What's with you? Are you angry at me for talking to those two for so long? I didn't want to, but their son has enrolled in Notre Dame and they just *had* to tell me all about it. I should have told them that I had this beautiful redhead who just happens to be my loving wife waiting for me—"

"Brady, are you ready to leave? I am." Finley snatched up her purse and pinned him with a direct stare, waiting for him to vacate the booth. She wanted to leave the restaurant because she suspected that the two gossipers were silent so that they could hear Bryan's words.

"It's Brady again, is it?" He tossed two bills on the table in a frustrated motion. "Okay, okay. Let's go."

While Bryan paid the check, Finley tried to place Anne. There were two choices. Anne Blackmoor, the wife of one of the team managers, or Anne Swinson, wife of the defensive coach. She decided it must be the latter. She'd seen Anne Swinson in the company of Tanya several times.

"I'm ready if you are. Want to do some more sightseeing?"

Finley shook her head. "I'm not feeling well. Let's go home."

"Not feeling well? What's wrong?"

Finley walked briskly to the car and didn't wait for Bryan to open her door. She slid into her seat and ignored his confused expression as he closed her door and went around the car to get in on the other side.

"I—I have a stomach ache," she lied.

"Oh." He started the engine. "Cramps?" Spots of pink found his cheeks as his own question embarrassed him.

Finley shrugged. "Yes." Let him think what he wants, she told herself. In fact, that's a nice excuse to hole up in my room and think things out.

She barely listened to his light banter as they drove home. Once inside, she excused herself and went to her bedroom. She lay across the bed and kicked off her shoes. Now! With a sigh, she let the bleak, black thoughts enter her mind.

In on a pass.

Those words sent a wave of fury and shame over her. How dare Tanya say that behind her back! She closed her eyes and wondered what, if anything, of the overheard conversation was true. Is Bryan still seeing Kristi? Before the party, Kristi had seemed quite at ease in asking Bryan—no, *expecting* Bryan—to be her escort. What was going on between them while she'd been playing sick after the wedding? Could

Bryan have made love to her so convincingly and be two-timing her?

A tortured moan escaped through her clenched teeth and Finley flopped over on her stomach and buried her face in the satin pillow cover.

Her earlier happiness seemed a flighty, foolish thing now. Obviously, Bryan's attitude had sparked Tanya's gossip. A shotgun wedding! Is that true? Finley felt her tears dampen the pillowcase. In a way, it *was* true. Nothing had changed, really, except that she'd fallen in love with Bryan Brady, but he had never vowed *his* love to her.

How ironic! She'd married Bryan to curb gossip and now gossip was making her miserable.

A light tapping at her door brought Finley to a sitting position. She grabbed a tissue and wiped her red-rimmed eyes as she asked, "Who's there?"

"Me, missus."

"Oh. Come in, Martha."

Martha's eyes widened slightly when she saw Finley's tear-streaked face. "The mister says you're not feeling good. You want an aspirin?" She held out her hand, displaying two tablets in her lined palm; she held a glass of water in the other hand.

Finley felt a dull ache behind her eyes and nodded. "Yes, thank you." She swallowed the aspirin, chasing them with water. "Where's Bryan?"

"He went to the gymnasium, missus. Says he'll be back this evening."

"Good." Finley lay back on the bed and closed her eyes. "I'll take my supper up here tonight, Martha."

"You having woman problems, missus?"

Finley smiled. "No, not really. I—I've just got a headache."

Martha cleared her throat. "No, missus. I mean, are you having woman problems that have to do with your man."

Finley opened her eyes in surprise. Martha had never interfered with her personal life! Had never even *hinted* at anything personal, and now she was asking if she'd had a row with Bryan?

"I—I don't know what you mean, Martha."

Martha shifted from one foot to another. "I just thought maybe you'd been crying because you'd had a fight with the mister. Me, I've been married for twenty-five years and I've had my quarrels with my man." She shrugged her heavy shoulders. "It's nothing to get so upset over, missus. Things will work out. Why, he'll probably bring flowers and candy home for you this evening."

Finley tried to smile. "Thank you for your concern, Martha."

Martha nodded and left the room, and Finley sighed and felt the tears threaten again. How she wished it were just a little spat as Martha assumed! Should she tell Bryan about the conversation she'd overheard? Should she confront him with it and demand to know if it were true or false?

That would be the adult thing to do, she told herself. He should at least be told what's troubling you! She sat up in the bed. She'd go to the gymnasium and tell him she had to speak with him. She'd discuss the situation openly and—and demand to know how she fits into his life. Finley nodded. Yes. She had to know if he loved her or not.

Finley went into the bathroom and took a quick shower. She dressed in gray wool slacks and a gray and white sweater, then applied lipstick and blusher and went downstairs. She felt better now that she'd filed a plan of action. This wondering about Bryan's true feelings just would not do! Somehow, she knew that Bryan would tell her he loved her and that Tanya was just a vicious gossip who didn't know a lie from the truth and probably didn't care.

Hadn't he told her he loved her in other ways? In the way he looked at her? In the way he touched her? In the way he'd murmured her name while he made love to her? Finley smiled to herself as she climbed into her car. Yes. He does love me, she thought. I know he does!

She drove past the Arkansas River and thought how gray

and unattractive it seemed without Bryan beside her. Of course, evening was approaching and the sun was buried beneath heavy, dark clouds while it had been brighter earlier that day and the mood had been merrier.

Parking the car in the back lot of the stadium complex, Finley noted the many cars and wondered if the players were getting nervous now and seeking the security of physical exertion. She entered the complex and was making her way down the corridor that led to the gymnasium when she caught the sound of Bryan's laughter. She paused and listened as his laughter sounded again, then she walked toward the sound. She edged closer to the office and glanced at the sign that read Wildcatters' Cheerleading Organization. Finley drew her brows together. What's he doing in there?

Carefully she moved to peek around the doorframe, then froze.

Kristi Sinclair stood in the office and her arms were around Bryan's neck. The young woman was smiling up into Bryan's face as his arms circled her waist.

"So, are you happy?" Bryan asked.

"Happy? You bet!" Kristi giggled. "This will be *our* little secret until after the Super Bowl, then we'll let everybody know."

Bryan chuckled and kissed Kristi's nose.

"Oh, Bryan! I can't wait until we can announce it!" Kristi stood on tiptoe to plant a brief kiss on Bryan's mouth. "I'm so happy."

Finley closed her eyes and backed from the doorway. She rested against the wall for a moment, her hands pressed against her stomach, then she walked robotlike back down the corridor and to the parking lot. She was barely conscious of unlocking the car, getting into it, and driving home. Only when she entered the entryway and saw Martha's concerned expression did she rouse herself from the trancelike state.

"Missus? What's wrong? Where'd you go? You—you're so pale! You sick again?"

Finley shook her head to all the questions and moved

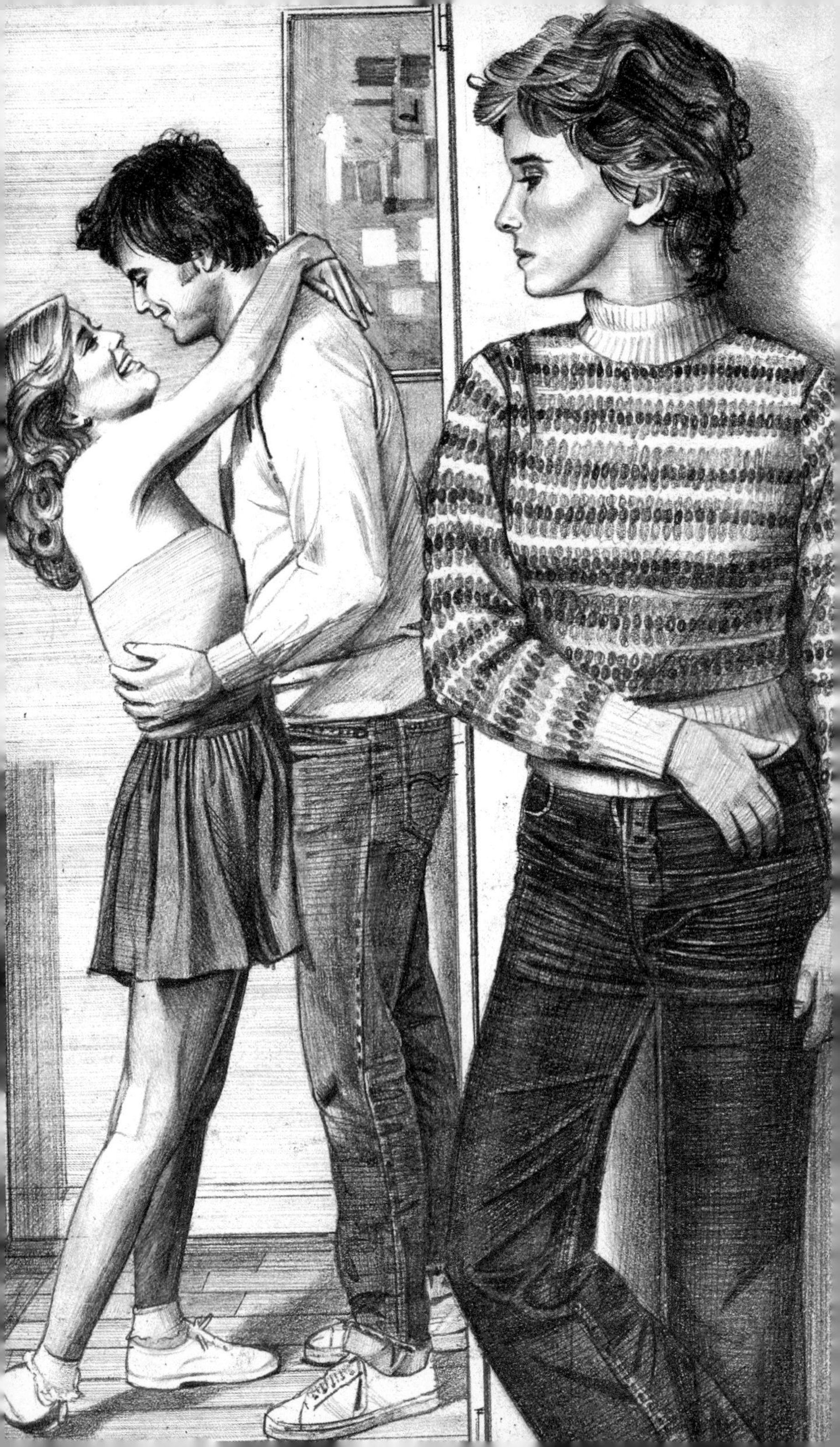

toward the staircase. "I'm fine, Martha. I'm going to my bedroom and rest for a while." She mounted the stairs and sought out the privacy of her bedroom.

Fool!

The word bounced back and forth in her mind and she closed her eyes and slumped into the chair by the window. And you thought he loved you! What a joke.

Tears spilled onto her cheeks and Finley swiped at them with the backs of her hands. So, Tanya was right. He's never stopped seeing Kristi and now—now they're planning to announce their engagement after the Super Bowl.

Well? Why not? That *was* the original plan! Bryan's marriage to her was only until after the Super Bowl and then they'd divorce and go their separate ways.

Finley rose from the chair and stumbled to the bed. She fell into its softness and closed her eyes. Exhaustion and the roller-coaster play of her emotions brought sleep immediately.

When she woke it was morning. Finley gasped when she saw that someone had slipped her under the covers sometime during the night. Martha? She hoped it had been her rather than Bryan. The thought of him touching her made her leap from the bed and stumble to the bathroom. She took a shower and dressed in jeans and a gold sweater.

During the night her dreams had come and gone and, somewhere, sometime, she had made a decision. Although her first impulse was to leave Bryan, she discarded the thought. She had made a commitment and she would stick to it. It was her own fault that she had assumed that just because she loved Bryan Brady he felt the same about her. Yes. She would stay and finish her internship as a photographer, but she would make it clear to Bryan that she didn't want him touching her.

Her head held high, Finley went into the kitchen and

found Bryan there alone. She balled her hands into tight fists and went to the cupboard for a cup.

"Good morning, Red. Feeling better?"

"Yes, thank you." She poured herself a cup of coffee and then turned to face him. "I must talk with you."

He gave her a quizzical look. "Okay. I'm listening."

"I—I've made a decision." She sipped the coffee, hoping it would give her a little strength. "I think we made a mistake in becoming too intimate. I've given it a lot of thought and I've decided it would be better if we treat this as just a—a—business arrangement."

"A business arrangement?" He set his cup down with a clatter. "What the hell are you talking about?"

Finley swallowed and straightened her spine. "I don't love you, Brady. I need to concentrate on my career and—and you're getting in the way. I think we should—" She swallowed the rest of her sentence with a gulp when she saw anger darken his eyes.

Bryan rose slowly from his chair and the cords in his neck stood out as evidence to the rage he was experiencing. His voice was a low growl. "What's this all about?"

Suddenly, she hated him for playing the part of the wounded party. She glared at him and was surprised at the hard edge to her voice. "If you'll stop interrupting me, I'll tell you! I let this situation run away with itself. We married for *convenience* and that—that incident the other night has caused me an inconvenience. I don't want you to think that I—I care for you. I'll keep up my end of the bargain but—but I don't want you touching me, except for appearances, of course."

"Are you finished?"

She cringed at his flat tone. "Yes."

"Very well." He let his gaze rake over her and his mouth thinned into a tight, white line. "And I thought you were different. But you're not, are you?" He drew a shaky breath and flexed his hands. "Thank you for setting me straight,

Red. Now that I know the score, I'll behave myself." He gave her a curt nod and turned on his heel. His stride was angry as he left the room. Moments later, the front door slammed.

Finley flinched at the sound, then collapsed in a nearby chair. She buried her face in her hands and thought she'd never forget the hurt and humiliation on his face. His pride's just hurt, she told herself. She recalled the first time she'd met him and how she'd wished she could be the first woman to drop him—to hurt him.

She laughed bitterly, then winced. Well, she'd gotten her wish. She'd shattered his pride. She should be proud of herself. She should be gloating over the fact that she'd seen through his mask of affection. But she wasn't.

Finley let the sobs shake her body until she felt as if she might be physically sick at any moment. Shame covered her body in a sticky blanket. She knew she'd never be able to forgive herself.

"It's not fair," she sobbed, then hiccuped. "Why can't he love me, too? Why does Kristi have to win?"

She rested her head on the tabletop and waited for the sobbing to subside. She'd have to get through the next few weeks, but she didn't know how she'd manage to do it.

11

Finley heard the telephone ring, but she didn't bother to answer it. She knew that Martha was downstairs with Bryan and one of them would get it. Without really looking at the contents, Finley browsed through a magazine and thought about Bryan as she had been doing for the past two weeks.

If he were seeing Kristi, she didn't know when or how he was managing it. With the Super Bowl approaching and the Wildcatters entering the final play-offs, Bryan was either drilling with the team, working out in the mini-gymnasium at home, or sleeping. Sometimes, late at night, Finley could hear him moving about downstairs, and once she had tiptoed downstairs to find him reading a football playbook. His eyes had been red-rimmed and lines of fatigue creased his face, and Finley had felt an almost uncontrollable desire to go to him and admit that her hasty speech about not wanting to be near him had been nothing but lies.

Several times since then she had wanted to tell him that she *did* love him; that she didn't want a divorce; that the very thought of leaving him made her feel ill. But then she would remember seeing his expression as he and Kristi made their secret plans, and she would call herself a fool. Bryan had looked so happy that day in the office with Kristi. Why can't he love me that way? Finley asked herself. Why can't he be happy with *me?*

Long days had melted into long nights following her scene

with him in the kitchen two weeks ago. Bryan never took meals in the dining room, preferring instead to eat by himself in his study or bedroom. Finley had lost all interest in food, sleeping, or even her photography. The joy of freezing seconds onto film was lost to her now, and she wondered if she'd ever regain enthusiasm for it or anything else again.

Finley closed the magazine and stretched out on her bed. She stared at the ceiling and found herself thinking of that day—it seemed so long ago now—when she had rested in Bryan's arms and felt like she belonged to him. Could he *really* have thought of her only as "one of his girls"? Could he have been thinking of Kristi while he made love to her?

Blinking away her tears, Finley sat up in bed when she heard a faint tapping at her door. "Yes?"

"Missus, the phone's for you. It's your dad."

"Oh. Thanks, Martha. I'll take it in here." Finley reached for the cream telephone on the bedside table. "Hello, Dad."

"Finley! Where have you been keeping yourself? I was just talking to Alicia, and we feel slighted. We haven't seen you or Bryan much these days."

"You see Bryan every day, Dad," Finley reminded him.

"Well, yes, but that's at work and we don't get to talk. Nothing's wrong, is it?"

Finley caught the worry in her father's voice. "No, nothing's wrong," she lied, wiping tears from her eyes but forcing her voice not to reveal her inner turmoil. "We've just been busy."

"Too busy to ask your old dad and Alicia over for Christmas dinner? You know, I miss your cooking."

Christmas! Finley closed her eyes. She knew Christmas was approaching, but she'd tried to avoid the subject. Dutifully, she'd done her Christmas shopping, but none of the usual merriment and anticipation had accompanied her this year. Guilt welled inside Finley when she realized that her father was right. She *had* been snubbing him and Alicia. She'd avoided everyone recently. But Christmas was a time for families. "I'm sorry, Dad. Why don't you and Alicia plan on having dinner with us as soon as you get back from the game Christmas night? What time do you think that'll be?"

"Oh, about eight o'clock. You aren't going to the game?"

"Uh–. No." Finley grappled for an excuse. "I–I have a lot to do to prepare for Christmas, and–I'll be cooking dinner!"

Her father chuckled. "That's right. Okay. We'll be there after the game and have a merry old Christmas."

"I'm looking forward to it, Dad. Good-bye now." Finley replaced the receiver and gave a shaky sigh. She'd have to tell Bryan, and that meant a confrontation—something she'd been avoiding for two weeks. A feeling of dread wormed its way inside her as she stood and made her way downstairs. A light was on in the study, and she knocked on the door.

"What is it, Martha?"

Finley opened the door and stuck her head inside the room. "It's not Martha. Can I come in for a minute?"

Bryan was sitting behind his desk, a playbook open in front of him. The remains of a dinner tray rested on top of the desk. He gave her a derisive look, then nodded toward a chair. "Sure. Have a seat."

Closing the door behind her, Finley took the seat offered and clasped her hands in her lap. She chided herself for feeling nervous and self-conscious in front of him.

"Well, what's on your mind? I'm kind of busy right now." His eyes were cold when he looked at her.

Finley cleared her throat and decided to try some small talk to see if she could erase the impatience from his face. "Are you studying the playbook for the play-offs?"

"Yes." He closed the book and leaned back in his chair. "Is *that* what you interrupted me for?"

She found she couldn't stand to look at him when he wore that impatient, cold expression, so she stared at her tightly clasped hands. "No, Dad just called and kind of invited himself and Alicia for dinner Christmas after the game. I was wondering if you'd be able to join us?"

"A friendly little family gathering, is that it?" His tone was mocking. "Do you think that's a good idea? They're bound to notice that we're not exactly crazy for each other."

Finley bit her bottom lip to keep it from trembling. "We'll have to do our best, Bryan. I—I couldn't get out of it." She turned pleading eyes on him. "Won't you *try?* I know you'll be tired after the game, but it is Christmas and it's just for one evening."

He shrugged his broad shoulders. "Okay, I'll try. I was never much good at acting, so be forewarned."

Finley relaxed and let out her pent-up breath. "Thank you. It might be pleasant, I mean having company and other people around for a change. We've been, well, sort of cooped up here lately."

"Are you saying you're not happy with the present arrangement?"

She looked at him, trying to read his taciturn expression. "I—Well, are you?"

His lids drooped to partially conceal his eyes from her. "No, but I've got things to keep me busy right now. Of course," his lids lifted, "you have your photography. Your career."

The last two words seemed to hold a sneer, and Finley looked at him in surprise. His mouth curved in a mocking smile.

"Yes, I have my career, but—"

"But?" he goaded her.

"One needs more than a career," Finley said, holding his gaze for a few seconds before he looked away.

"I agree." He placed his hands flat on the desk and straightened in his chair. "But right now I've got work to do, so if that's all you had on your mind. . . ?"

Finley felt as if she'd been pushed off a cliff. For some reason she'd felt close to some admission, some insight to Bryan's moods. But now the door was closed again. Now she was back in her dark abyss, alone and confused. He was opening the playbook again and Finley stood up and started to leave the room, but his voice stopped her at the door.

"What time are they coming Christmas night?"

"Eight," she told him over her shoulder.

"Okay." He bowed his head over the book, dismissing her.

Finley stared at his bent head for a few seconds, wanting desperately to feel his hair between her fingers and his lips upon hers. With a sigh, she wrenched open the door and then slammed it behind her.

Standing before the full-length mirror in her bedroom, Finley arranged a cluster of white orchids in her hair. She stepped back from the mirror and examined her white bare-shouldered dress, rubbing her hands down the rich silk texture. Finley liked the way the dress clung to her breasts from thin straps and then fell loosely in soft, feminine folds. She clasped her necklace of gold and emeralds around her neck, and wondered if she might be overdressed. She shook her head at the thought. It had been weeks since she'd had an opportunity to dress up and it might be weeks before she'd get another chance. Besides, it was Christmas and the Wildcatters had won another game today. The Super Bowl was a sure thing now. She'd watched the game on television, her gaze constantly searching for Bryan. Pride had consumed her as the announcers doused Bryan with praise. For a few minutes she had basked in the knowledge that she was his wife, then the spell had been broken as she recalled the memory of him kissing Kristi.

She pushed the thoughts from her mind. It was Christmas, and she yearned to let herself go and forget her troubles just for one night. She glanced toward the window and watched the snowflakes fall onto the pane only to melt into glistening drops.

Fingering the emeralds, Finley smiled and thought of her mother, a woman she could barely remember. These jewels had been her mother's, given to her by her father on their first anniversary. After her mother's death her father had kept them until Finley was eighteen, and then presented them to her.

"Every Irish lassie should have emeralds to show off her red hair and ivory complexion," he'd told her.

Looking at her image in the mirror, Finley realized that she favored her mother. The same hair, same eyes, same build, and now the same emeralds. The jewels must have been her father's most lavish gift, a gift to be passed on for generations.

Finley pulled herself from her reflections and left her room. She was entering the living room to make sure everything was tidy when the doorbell chimed and she went to greet her father and Alicia.

"Welcome," Finley said, taking Alicia's coat. "You look lovely, Alicia." Finley admired the woman's blue, simply cut gown. It was casual but sleek and sophisticated. Her father was dressed in a dark suit and she smiled at him as he tugged at his bow tie. "Daddy, you look so handsome. Here, now you've messed up your tie." She straightened it for him and kissed his ruddy cheek. "You certainly need someone to look after you. Alicia will have a full-time job."

Her father frowned good-naturedly and Alicia laughed and linked her arm in his. "It's a job I'll relish, Finley."

Finley felt tears of self-pity sting her eyes. They're so happy, she thought as she led her father and Alicia into the living room. That's the way it should be but never can be for Bryan and me. Kristi won't let that happen. She's got Bryan wrapped around her finger!

"Good evening. My, don't we look nice tonight. How about a drink?"

Finley stared at Bryan, surprised to find him in the living room. She'd assumed he was still upstairs dressing. His broad shoulders were emphasized by the dark suit he wore and his hair gave off a coppery sheen in the lamplit room. A pale blue shirt and blue and black striped tie drew attention to his cool blue eyes. Why does he have to be so good-looking? Finley wondered grimly. It would be easier to let him go if he weren't so attractive! Will I ever find someone else to fill his shoes? To fill this void he's left in me?

"What will it be, Finley?"

She blinked, then shoved her doubts aside and answered him. "Just a ginger ale for me, thanks."

He raised an eyebrow, then shrugged. "Afraid I'll get you drunk tonight?"

His barbed words found their target and Finley felt them prick her heart. She swallowed and lowered her gaze, refusing to let him see how he'd hurt her. Mike Malone and Alicia settled on the couch and Finley perched on a chair. Her nerves were taut, her stomach tying itself into knots. Accepting the drink from Bryan, she made sure not to touch Bryan's lean fingers. She sipped the drink and only half-listened to the casual conversation, hating the way Bryan seemed so comfortable and in control of himself. Why shouldn't he be? she asked herself. Everything's going his way. He's heading for the Super Bowl. He's got the comforts of a temporary family and has a *real* lover waiting in the wings. Finley glanced around the spacious living room and realized with a pang that this wouldn't be her home too much longer. She'd grown to love the house and had even toyed with decorating ideas. A bitter smile found her lips. Kristi would have to decorate the place.

"Hey, let's open presents!"

Finley looked up in surprise at Bryan's announcement. He stood and crossed to the Christmas tree, hauling out the presents beneath and distributing them. Bryan handed Finley a red-and-white-wrapped present. She hadn't seen it before and she looked at the card.

"Dad! Alicia! How did you?"

Her father laughed. "Bryan brought them home with him this evening. He slipped them under the tree for us."

With trembling fingers, she unwrapped the gift and gasped

when she saw the pale blue satin nightdress with its matching coverlet.

"Oh, it's beautiful." She stood and kissed her father and Alicia. "Look, Bryan." She held it up in front of her and turned to face him.

A look of longing found his eyes as he gazed at the intimate article of clothing, then his eyes lifted to find her flushed face. Finley trembled as her blood caught fire from the spark in his eyes, and she hastily dropped the gift back into its box and turned from his frank expression. She was grateful that Alicia and her father were occupied with opening presents and didn't see the play of emotions.

Her father grinned and held up his cowboy hat with its fancy feather band. "Well, will you look at this?"

Finley laughed. "Now you're a real Oklahoma cowboy, Dad. Do you like it?"

"I love it." He placed a hand on her cheek and stroked it lovingly.

"Oh, look, Mike!" Alicia lifted the silver serving tray from the box and pointed to the inscription. "It says, 'Mike and Alicia Malone, The Second Time Around.'" Alicia's eyes filled with tears. "Thank you, Finley and Bryan."

Bryan kissed her cheek. "Just a little early wedding present." He turned quickly toward Finley and tossed a present into her lap. "Here, Red." He glanced at the last gift. "Is that for me?"

"Yes." Finley's hands closed around the candy-striped bow on the present and she could feel her father's eyes on her as she carefully unwrapped the gift. She paused as Bryan opened his present and smiled when pleasure blanketed his face.

He lifted the bronze statue of a quarterback from the box to examine it. The quarterback was standing, his feet braced, his arm cocked to hurl the football into the air. Bryan's eyes widened.

"It's got my number! Ten!"

Finley nodded. "I found it at Alicia's gallery."

A wistful smile settled on his mouth and he moved to set the statue on the mantle. "Thanks, Red." It was a whisper, and it filled Finley with a need to feel his arms around her on this special day. He turned quickly from the mantle. "Well, open yours."

She batted away the sentiment and lifted the lid of the box. Her hands wrestled with the designer camera case and the scent of leather surrounded her. The case was large enough to hold two or three cameras, film, and other equipment and it was feminine and stylish, quite different from her old bulky one. Bryan cleared his throat and Finley looked up into his eyes.

"It's lovely," she said quietly as she handed it to her dad for inspection. "My other one is so old and worn."

"I noticed." Bryan's expression suddenly turned cold. "It should help you in your—career."

Finley flinched at his barb and was relieved when Martha announced that dinner was ready to serve. Quickly, she stood and walked with the others into the dining room to sit down to the meal she had prepared. The ham, vegetables, hot rolls, and traditional cranberry mold was lost on her, though; her appetite was gone now that her stomach was churning with nerves and tension. She smiled as her father kept complimenting her on the meal, showing his appreciation by taking a second helping.

"Don't know how you keep your weight down, Bryan," her father said with a chuckle. "With meals like this, I'd gain sixty pounds in one week!"

Bryan smiled and pushed his empty plate aside. "She is a good cook, but I spend hours in the gym working off these meals, Coach."

Finley glanced at him. What meals? They hadn't dined together in weeks. If he ate at home he ate in privacy, and she had no idea what his meals consisted of since Martha prepared them. He'd never asked her to cook for him.

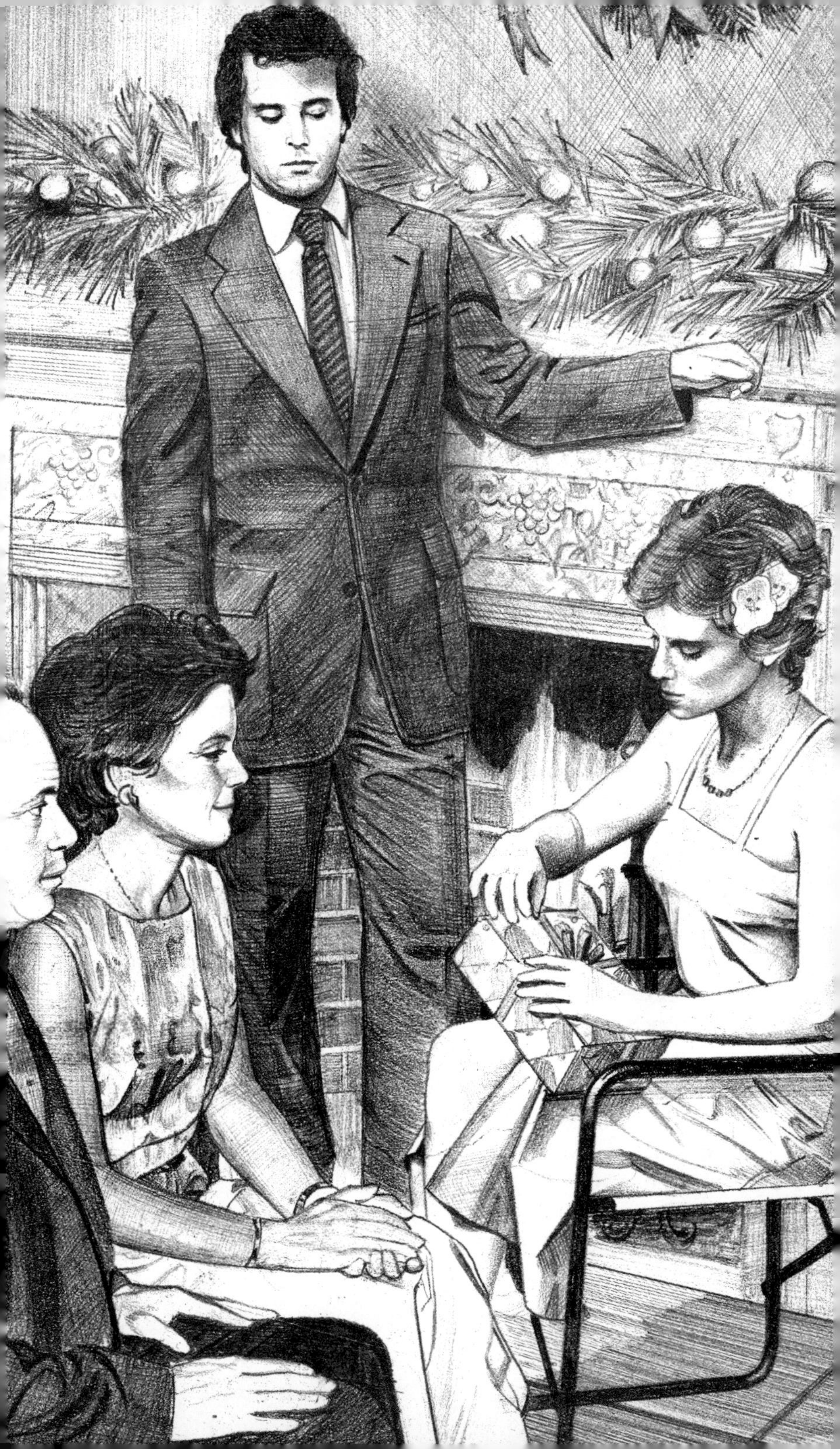

She shrugged mentally. He's playing a part—the part of a happy, contented husband—for her father's benefit.

"Alicia and I have set a date, Finley."

"Oh?" Finley looked at her father. "When?"

"The Sunday following the Super Bowl. Would you help Alicia with the wedding plans?"

"Of course." Finley gave Alicia a warm smile.

"You'll be my matron of honor, won't you?"

"I'd be honored, Alicia." Finley reached across the table to squeeze her stepmother-to-be's hand.

"And Bryan? You'll be the best man?" Alicia asked.

Finley tensed and removed her hand from Alicia's, afraid her reaction would be telegraphed to the other woman.

"Of course, I will, Alicia. I'm honored, coach."

"Well, you *are* my son-in-law and I'm proud of that fact, I don't mind telling you." Mike Malone grinned and winked at Bryan.

A clammy film of perspiration covered Finley and she leaned back in the chair. What did Bryan think he was doing, accepting a part in the marriage party? Was he intending to bring Kristi along as his date? She looked at him, seated next to her, a happy smile on his lips. Is he really so untouched by all of this, or is he a fantastic actor? she wondered.

"There won't be very much to arrange, Finley. It's going to be a rather private ceremony; nothing big."

Finley pulled her eyes away from her husband and nodded at Alicia. "Just let me know how I can help."

"We'll go out next week and pick out dresses; is that okay?"

"Fine." Finley gulped some wine and noticed that her hand was shaking. She clutched her hands in her lap and took some deep breaths to try to calm her nerves.

"Why not have your reception here?"

"Here?" Finley turned to Bryan, her eyes wide with pain and panic. "I—I don't think that's a good idea. We should have the reception at Dad's."

"Why?" Bryan asked her, his brows meeting in a scowl. "They won't be able to sneak off and leave their guests at their own home. I insist we have the reception here."

"Bryan!" Finley's voice was a low warning, an urgent plea.

Mike Malone cleared his throat. "Maybe we should have it at our house. We're leaving early that evening for the South Pacific."

"Nonsense!" Bryan frowned at Finley, then looked at the coach. "It would be easier to have it here, then you won't have to worry about cleaning up after it. You go on your honeymoon and Finley and I will tie up the loose ends while you two are having fun in the sun."

Cold realization washed over Finley and she slumped in her chair. So that's it! He's going to wait until after the wedding to drop the bomb on our marriage, she thought. By the time Dad gets back from his honeymoon the loose ends—our marriage—will be taken care of and Bryan won't have to go through all this with Dad breathing down his neck!

She stared at Bryan Brady and wondered how he could be so cold and calculating. His blue eyes found hers and widened a fraction at the mask of fury on her face.

"Don't you agree, Finley?"

Finley lifted her chin slightly. "Yes. It makes perfect sense—now."

His eyes narrowed at her words and she saw confusion enter their blue depths. Don't act innocent with me, she thought. I know what you're up to!

The play of tension in the room must have reached Mike and Alicia because they both shifted uncomfortably in their chairs. Bryan tore his eyes from Finley and pushed back his chair.

"Let's take this party back to the living room where we can be comfortable," he suggested, and Mike and Alicia rose almost gratefully from their chairs to follow him.

Finley joined them and sat in a chair near the fireplace and watched the flames there sputter and spit. She barely listened to the conversation, only commenting when questions were directed at her. Her mind was numb with pain, and she refused to cast her thoughts ahead to her future.

"You remember that play, don't you, Finley?" Her father asked. "Didn't you take a picture of it?"

"What play?" Finley tried to catch the train of conversation.

Her father looked exasperated with her. "The winning touchdown last week in Texas. The quarterback sneak."

"Quarterback sneak?" Finley repeated, trying to recall.

"Quarterback sneak," Bryan said patiently. "You know what that is, don't you?"

Venom tasted bitter on Finley's tongue as she turned to her husband and gave him a hard smile. "Yes. I know all about how sneaky quarterbacks can be."

Bryan's eyebrows met and his mouth thinned into an angry, white line. A muscle jerked in his jaw and he drew a deep, shaking breath.

"Uh." Mike cleared his throat. "Anyway, it was a great play, don't you agree, Finley?"

Finley shrugged. "I guess."

"You guess," Bryan said, his voice dry and brittle.

Finley snapped her head in his direction and her voice was a whip. *"I'm* not the one who's into game playing, Brady. *You* are!"

"Finley, girl! What's going on?" Mike frowned and ignored Alicia's cautioning hand on his arm. "Have you two been fighting?"

Immediately, Finley was contrite and ashamed at her outburst. She looked at her father's worried face and wished she hadn't displayed her emotions so clearly in front of him.

"No, Coach." Bryan's voice was even, controlled. "It's just been a hectic few weeks for us. The Super Bowl is getting to us. You understand."

Mike Malone seemed to hesitate a moment, then he nodded and smiled. "Sure, sure. It gets to all of us, I guess."

He touched Alicia's hand. "Guess we'd better go. I've got a busy day tomorrow, and so do you, Bryan."

"Right, but I'm glad you came over tonight. We should have invited you weeks ago." Bryan stood and started toward the door.

Feeling a strange mixture of anger and gratitude, Finley followed them to the foyer. She was angry at Bryan for his cool, unperturbed handling of the evening and grateful for his quick intervention in glossing over her outburst. She kissed her dad good night and promised to call Alicia early next week to arrange a shopping engagement.

When the last good-byes had been said, Bryan closed the front door and leaned against it. His eyes bored into Finley, who stood nervously a few feet from him.

"Mind telling me what's on your mind, Red? Or do you like playing this game and keeping me in the dark?"

"Keeping *you* in the dark?" Finley gasped at his gall. *"I'm the one in the dark."*

"Oh? Then why am I so confused? I haven't the slightest idea why you behaved so rudely tonight. What have I done? Haven't I left you alone to pursue your career? I've kept out of your way, haven't I? So, what's the problem?"

She glared at him, her hands balled into fists and itching to pound his solid chest. "How could you have accepted a part in Dad's wedding when you know you won't be part of my family for long?"

He narrowed his eyes in a menacing way that sent shivers along Finley's spine. "Regardless of how long I remain in your family, I have a lot of respect for your father. He's my coach and my friend and I have every right to be his best man at his wedding."

"It's all such a sham!" Finley's eyes filled with tears and she turned her back on Bryan.

"Our marriage might be a sham but my friendship with your father isn't." He drew a deep breath and whispered her name. "Finley, Finley." His hands closed over her shoulders, warmth enveloping her.

Finley felt her knees grow weak and she longed to lean back against him but his deceit surfaced in her mind and she straightened and spun from him. "Don't touch me!"

His hands dropped to his sides and his eyes glazed with icy anger. "Okay, okay!" His gaze raked over her, taking in her shaking figure. "I'm going to bed." He brushed past her and mounted the stairs three at a time.

Finley closed her eyes, listening to his angry-sounding footsteps and the slamming of his bedroom door.

Why can't I hate him, she wondered and her heart ached. *Why can't I hate him?*

Finley fell onto the sofa and kicked off her pumps. She wiggled her toes and looked wearily at the pyramid of boxes on the floor near her.

A full day of shopping with Alicia had left her limp and exhausted, but it had kept her from thinking of Bryan. Alicia had tried to pry information from Finley as to her current situation with the team's quarterback, but Finley had been reluctant to talk to Alicia. Why burden Alicia with dark problems on the eve of her wedding? Finley had steered the conversation to safe waters and forced a cheeriness she didn't feel.

The doorbell chimed, and Finley moaned and started to rise from the sofa.

"I'll get it, missus."

"Oh, thanks, Martha." Finley relaxed, closing her eyes and listening as Martha opened the door.

"Missus? It's Mrs. Gena."

"Gena?" Finley propped herself on her elbows and smiled at her friend. "Come in, Gena. You don't mind if I don't rise to my aching feet, do you?"

Gena smiled. "No, you look exhausted." Gena eyed the boxes. "On a shopping spree?"

Finley shook her head. "I've been buying an outfit for

Dad's wedding. I'm the matron of honor." Finley looked at Martha who stood in the doorway. "Could we have some tea, Martha?"

Martha nodded and went to prepare the tea tray.

"Can I take a peek?" Gena asked, already opening the boxes and plucking out the contents. "Oh, this is beautiful!" She held up a peach-colored pillbox hat with a sheer veil. "And this!" She lifted a matching peach dress from the next box. "I bet this color looks smashing on you."

"Alicia's wearing a cream-colored dress with peach trim. It's lovely, too. Heavens, I thought we'd never satisfy her! We went all over Tulsa and I think we hit every shop."

Gena laughed and folded the dress back into the box. "When's the big day?"

"Sunday after the Super Bowl. You'll get an invitation any day. Gena, would you help me with the reception? We're having it here and I could use your help in serving the guests. Would you mind?"

"No, not at all." Gena sat down in the chair opposite the sofa.

"Thanks. I think Martha and I will have our hands full and I thought about hiring extra help, but . . ."

Gena shook her head. "No need to do that. We can manage. Is it going to be a big wedding?"

"No, just close friends and a few relatives." Finley sighed and wiggled her tired toes. "Bryan insisted on having the reception here."

"You didn't want to?"

"I don't mind hosting the reception, I just didn't want it to be held here."

"Why not?"

Finley sat up as Martha entered the room with the tea tray. She put the tray on the coffee table and poured the tea.

"Thank you, Martha."

Martha eyed the parcels. "Want me to hang those up, missus?"

"Yes, would you?"

The woman nodded and gathered the boxes, then left the room.

Gena smiled. "I don't know why, but I like her. Does she ever smile?"

Finley laughed. "Seldom, if ever. Here, have a cookie."

Gena acepted one of the cookies, then leaned back in her chair and pinned Finley with a curious stare. "You want to talk about it?"

"About what?" Finley sipped the hot tea and wondered if she were transparent.

"About whatever's bothering you. Finley, you look absolutely washed out and shopping can't be the only reason. You haven't called me in weeks. What's the problem? Bryan?"

Finley sighed. "So, you know about Bryan?"

"What about him?"

"That he's going to marry Kristi as soon as the Super Bowl is over."

"What?" Gena sat straighter in the chair. "Did *he* say that?"

Finley shrugged. "He didn't have to. I heard him making plans with Kristi. It seems I'm the last to know."

"No, *I'm* the last to know," Gena corrected her. "I had no idea that that was still going on."

"Well, everyone else knows. I overheard two of the wives talking about it in a restaurant." Finley's mouth dipped in a bitter frown as she recalled the catty, hateful conversation.

"Wait, wait!" Gena leaned forward. "Start at the beginning. You've lost me."

Finley took a deep, shaking breath and told Gena about the overheard conversation in the restaurant and about Bryan and Kristi's plans. Throughout the narrative Gena's expression became more and more troubled, but she made no comment until Finley had finished.

Silence commanded the room for several minutes until Gena finally poured herself another cup of tea and shook her head, her expression a mixture of sadness and confusion.

"Well, I just don't believe it," she said with determination.

"You don't believe it?" Finley asked, shocked. "Why not? It makes sense to me."

"Not to me." Gena rested in the chair and stirred her tea thoughtfully. "Jilly has mentioned that Bryan's been uptight lately, but we all figured it was because of the Super Bowl. There's been no gossip about him and Kristi. In fact, he barely speaks to Kristi, or so Jilly tells me." Gena sipped her tea, then set the cup down with a bang. "No, it just doesn't add up, Finley. Something's wrong."

"But I heard the wives—"

"Oh, those two." Gena wrinkled her nose in disgust. "They're always stirring up trouble."

"But you said they were usually right," Finley reminded her.

"*Usually* right, but they're wrong this time. I know Kristi's seeing someone, but I don't think it's Bryan."

Finley smiled bitterly. "It's Bryan. He's *never* home. Gena, I saw them! I *heard* them talking about making their announcement right after the Super Bowl in January."

Gena's eyes softened to a velvety brown as she looked at Finley. "Finley, do you love him?"

Finley's bottom lip trembled and she crumpled into tears. "Yes, yes." She sobbed and hid her face in her hands, ashamed at breaking down in front of her friend.

Gena was beside her on the sofa in a flash, her arms encircling Finley. "Honey, honey, don't you worry," she whispered, letting Finley sob on her shoulder. "Why not turn a deaf ear on all this and just wait it out? Wait until after the Super Bowl when Bryan's head is on straight, and then just clear the air."

Finley shook her head. "H-he doesn't l-love me."

"I think you're wrong, Finley. I don't think he knows what he wants right now, other than a Super Bowl championship ring. Let him get that out of his system, then make him talk to you."

"It'll be too late," Finley said, wiping the tears from her

cheeks. "He's going to announce his engagement right after the game."

"No he won't. Why, he'd be crazy to announce his engagement while he's still married! Take it from someone who knows, honey. That man's got only one thing on his mind and that's football. When the season's over you'll have your chance to make him confront his relationship with you."

Finley tried to laugh. "What relationship?"

Gena grasped Finley's left hand and lifted it so that her wedding ring caught the light. "That ring signifies that you've got a hold on that man, Finley. That ring means he *has* to listen to you. Kristi or no Kristi, *you're* his wife."

A smile that threatened to dissolve at any second curved Finley's mouth. "Okay, Gena. Thanks for listening."

"Hey, what are friends for?" She patted Finley's hand. "Now, let's have our tea and cookies."

Finley nodded and sipped her tea. She looked at Gena and thought what a good friend she had become. She's right, Finley thought. There's nothing I can do about it now.

"H-how do you know Kristi's seeing someone, Gena?" she asked after a moment.

Gena shrugged. "She's got that 'I'm in love' look about her." Gena gave Finley a stern look. "But that doesn't mean it's Bryan she's in love with, Finley."

Finley lowered her lashes and bit back her retort. It is Bryan, she thought. I know that look. I've had it myself.

12

New Orleans was filled with football fans. The stadium acted as a magnet to those who wanted to see in person the final football game of the season and the season's victors.

Finley wandered along the sideline, feeling as if she could reach out and touch the tense anticipation that hovered in the air. She gazed up at the bleachers for a few moments, watching the first ticketholders scramble for their seats, then she walked to a low bench and began checking out her camera equipment. An army of photographers were doing the same thing around her. She could hear the clicks of shutters, the whine of flash units, and the sound of zippers being zipped on camera cases.

Checking the amount of light in the stadium with her light meter, Finley made a mental note of it and set her camera's shutter speed and f-stop. Though she knew she appeared calm and composed on the outside, a jumble of conflicting emotions stirred within her. Anticipation mingled with dread and excitement fought to control an utter sense of desolation inside her. She knew she would always recall this game with a smile and a wince, for this Super Bowl marked both a beginning and an ending for her—the beginning of a career as a professional sports photographer and the end of her marriage to Bryan Brady.

She twisted her wedding ring around on her finger and smiled half-heartedly at a passing photographer with the opposing Florida team. A spatter of applause brought her around to face the bleachers and she saw a group of people pointing to someone on the sidelines. Finley turned in the direction of their gestures and saw Bryan striding toward her, his head down. Behind him a television reporter and cameraman were gathering their equipment, having finished an interview with Bryan. Finley clutched the camera in her hands for support as she watched Bryan draw closer to her. When he was just a few feet from her, he glanced up and his steps slowed as his gaze locked on her. He wasn't in his uniform yet and he looked lean and athletic in snug blue jeans and a sweatshirt that proclaimed "Wildcatter Signal Caller." Suddenly, Finley remembered the first time she'd met him and of her mental jest of calling him a perfect ten. At that time, she had thought it funny but now her heart twisted at the memory because he had become almost perfect to her; almost perfect *for* her. With a dull ache near her heart, she wondered if she'd ever find another man who could release in her such raging passion.

Hungrily, her gaze swept his face and she noted the tense set of his mouth, the dark intensity of his eyes, and the determined thrust of his chin. He looked like a coiled spring, and Finley realized that he was mentally preparing himself for the duel ahead of him.

"Hello," he said as he approached her to stand just at her side. "I've been looking for my folks and I just got word that they've been detained."

"Oh?" Finley swallowed the lump of emotion in her throat. "Are they going to get here in time to see the game?"

"Yes." He shoved his hands into the back pockets of his jeans. "You can meet them at the victory party. Okay?"

Finley nodded, almost smiling at his confidence in himself and his team. Victory party. He would consider nothing else. His words sunk into her numb brain and she winced inwardly at his suggestion that she meet his parents. I won't be

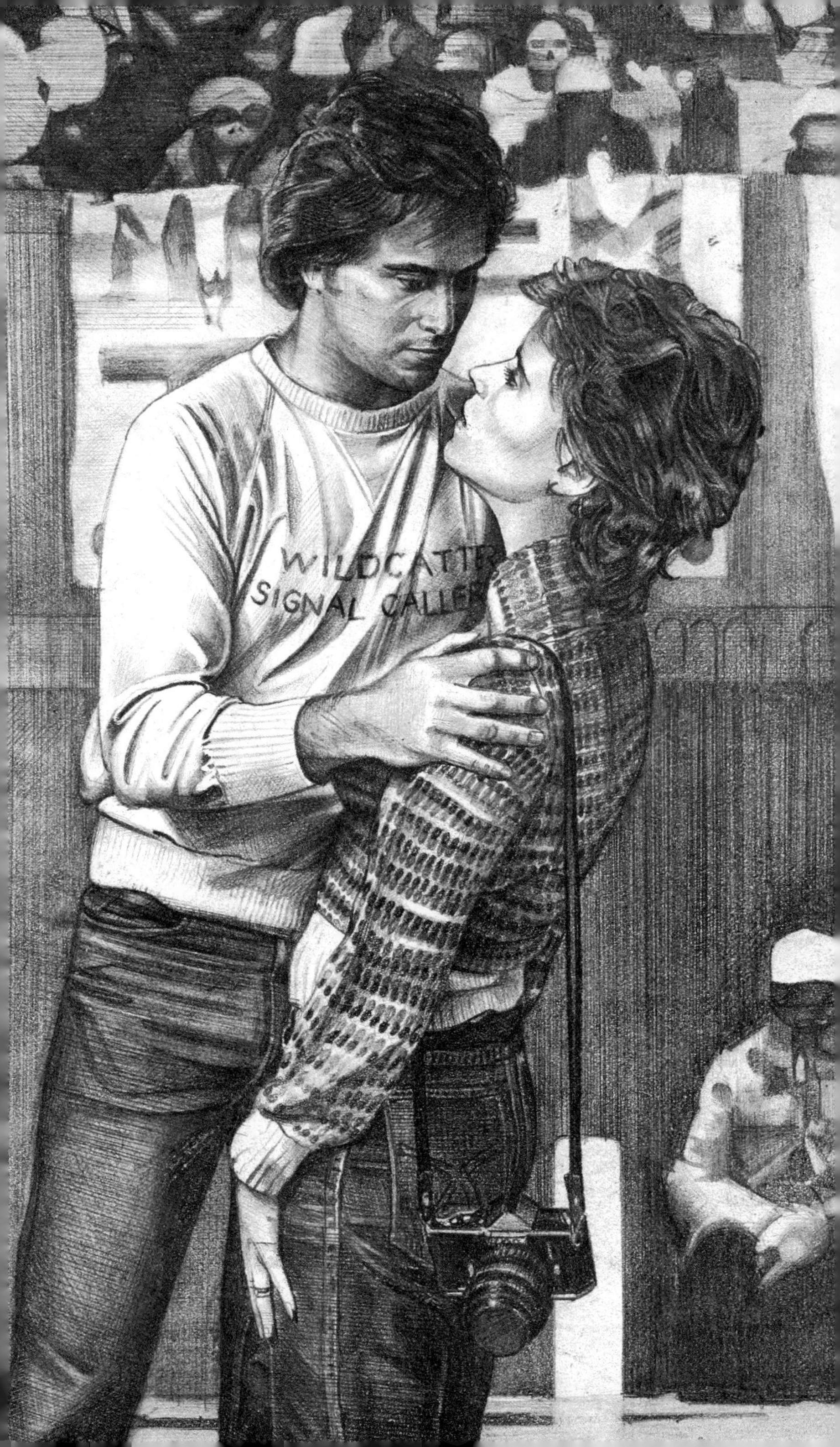
WILDCATT
SIGNAL CALLE

there, she thought. I'm leaving you right after this game. I can't play by your rules anymore, Bryan.

He shifted his weight from one foot to another and seemed at a loss for words. Finally, his eyes found hers, and for a few seconds, Finley found herself staring at those eyes and watching a play of emotions that were too complicated for her to decipher. Then he leaned forward and planted a quick kiss on her cheek.

"Good luck today, Finley." He smiled. "Take some good pictures of me, okay?"

He started to walk away but Finley reached out and grasped his arm. Without thinking past her need to touch him, to feel the pressure of his lips once more upon hers, to press her soft body against the hardness of his, Finley stood on tiptoes and raked her mouth across his in a desperate final kiss.

"Good luck, Bryan. Win this one for—for—" She pulled away from him, her courage deserting her and drying the last word on her tongue: me.

"Win this for?" His eyes teased her. "For you, Red?"

She couldn't look at him and her bottom lip trembled as his soft voice seemed to caress her. She tensed as his hands gripped her shoulders to turn her to face him again.

"I *will* win this one for you, Red." His mouth found hers in a crushing, tantalizing kiss that made her head spin with conflicting signals. His lips were deliciously warm on hers, a perfect fit, as they moved over hers, teasing them apart for a moment so that he could taste the warmth within. Too soon, the kiss was over and he was staring deep into her eyes. "And thanks, Finley. I needed that." His mouth curved in a charming smile, a smile that seemed to brighten Finley's world, flooding it with yellow and gold and amber.

Finley stood trembling on the brink of some soul-shaking realization as he strode past her and made his way to the stadium tunnel that led to the team dressing rooms. She closed her eyes and whispered, "I love you," to the place he had stood a moment before. "I love you and I don't know how I'm going to find the courage to give you up, but I will."

When she opened her eyes it was to focus on Kristi Sinclair. The other woman sat on the grassy sidelines and Finley knew she must have viewed the entire scene, but the naked jealousy Finley expected wasn't evident on Kristi's face. The cheerleader was actually smiling at Finley, a sentimental smile that disconcerted Finley for a moment, then Finley understood its meaning.

Why would Kristi be jealous? She knows she has Bryan. Her time with him is just beginning, Finley thought.

Kristi stood and walked toward Finley and Finley resisted the urge to turn and walk in the other direction. Instead, Finley watched the flash of Kristi's long legs under her short, pleated skirt and the way the other woman's blond hair contrasted nicely with her tanned skin.

"Hi," Kristi said, still smiling. "I guess Bryan is pretty uptight right now."

"Y-yes, I suppose so." Finley eyed the woman warily, waiting for the barbed words to begin.

Kristi extended a hand to Finley. "Good luck, Finley. I know this is an important day for you—careerwise, I mean."

Finley stared at the woman's extended hand in shock. Almost of its own accord, her hand clasped Kristi's in a brief handshake. "T-thank you."

Kristi shrugged, then her eyes sparkled. "Are you coming to the victory party? Oh, of course you are. Well, I'm going to announce something pretty important, so I thought I'd just forewarn you." Kristi smiled, her dimples deepening in her cheeks.

Finley drew back her hand as if she'd been burned. An announcement? She felt her face flame as she stared at the other woman and wondered how anyone could be so rude, so unfeeling.

Kristi gave her a curious glance, then turned to look over

her shoulder at the other cheerleaders. "I've got to go and warm up. See you later." She turned and trotted toward the cheerleaders who were practicing a routine.

Finley drew a deep, calming breath and blinked away the film of tears. One thing she wouldn't miss about all of this was Kristi Sinclair, she thought. She'd be glad to have that woman out of her life forever.

The game raced by in a blur of colors, sounds, feelings, and, finally, sweet success for Finley. Fighting for position on the sidelines with the other photographers, Finley was surprised at her own aggressiveness and sense of professionalism. Through most of the game she was able to forget that her husband was on that field, but once in a while she'd find him standing near her on the sidelines and the hurt of losing him would come back to her, full force.

In the third quarter of the game, Finley stood with her booted feet planted firmly in the sideline turf and was intent on capturing a shot of a charging player. She clicked the shutter button just as the massive player stormed to the sidelines, hotly pursued by two Wildcatters, and brushed against Finley. The force of the two-hundred-pound-plus body against Finley's sent her stumbling back a few steps before she was caught in a steel grip. She turned her head to thank her rescuer, then sucked in her breath when she saw Bryan. His blue eyes shone with concern.

"Are you okay, Finley?"

She gulped and nodded, righting herself and edging out of his grasp.

"Okay." He lifted his helmet and positioned it on his head. "But be careful, sweetheart. You could have been hurt."

She watched him trot onto the field, stunned by his words and the endearment. *Sweetheart.* Her heart tumbled over itself and she couldn't keep the happy smile from her lips. He hadn't said it with a sneer, but with a note of sincerity. She stubbornly closed her mind and her heart to the hope that was welling there, calling herself a foolish, lovesick woman who was grasping at straws in the wind.

It's over, she told herself as the last buzzer sounded to designate the Wildcatters as the champions by a ten-point margin. *It's over:* But she wasn't referring to the game.

Finley moved about the hotel room in a daze, automatically taking clothes from hangers and folding them into her open suitcase on the double bed. The ache in her heart was gone now, replaced by a void that worried her. She wondered if she'd ever be able to feel anything again, if she'd ever be able to cry again.

Upon her arrival in her hotel room, Finley had given way to racking sobs and bitter tears. Now, her eyes red-rimmed and slightly swollen, she was in control of herself again. She glanced at her watch, and alarm shook her when she realized that more than an hour had passed since she'd arrived at the hotel. Quickly, she threw the rest of her things into the suitcase and closed it. She let her gaze sweep the room once more, making certain she'd left nothing, then went to the telephone to call for a porter.

She froze when the door swung open and Bryan Brady stood on the threshold, his face set in a hard, stubborn mask.

"Bryan! W-what are you doing here?" She replaced the receiver and clasped her hands in front of her.

"So, you really are leaving me, aren't you?" He closed the door behind him and folded his arms across his wide chest.

Finley thought he looked dark and foreboding in the navy blue suit, white shirt, and dark tie. She swallowed and glanced at her suitcase. "Yes, I'm leaving."

"My parents are waiting to meet you at the party. What am I supposed to tell them?"

Finley adopted his pose, trying to look composed and indifferent. "They're *your* parents. You'll think of something."

"Thanks for the vote of confidence." He moved from the door to stand at the end of the bed. "Everyone's asking for you at the party. You missed Kristi's announcement."

Finley laughed, a brittle sound. "I didn't miss anything, then." She smoothed the skirt of her burgundy dress and wished he would leave her be.

"Yes, you *did* miss something. I thought you'd be surprised when she announced her engagement to Rick Waverly."

Finley stepped back, her composure slipping away. "What? Rick Waverly!"

Bryan's eyes were a dark cobalt blue as he looked at her and his voice was soft, but with a hard edge to it. "Yes. Rick Waverly."

"But—but I thought . . ."

"I know. I talked with Gena."

"Gena?" Finley's heart climbed into her throat and feelings flooded through her again, making her cheeks flush and her breath come in quick gasps. "Bryan, I saw you and Kristi at the stadium. I heard you—"

"You heard us discussing Kristi's engagement secret, yes. She wanted to keep it hush-hush until after the Super Bowl when things were back to normal for the team. We were discussing her engagement to Rick!"

Finley pressed her hands to either side of her face. "I—I had no idea. How long have they been dating? This is awfully sudden!"

A smile tugged at Bryan's mouth. "Not so sudden. I know from experience that a person can fall in love fast and hard, before he even knows what's happening to him."

Hope burned in Finley's soul as she listened to him. "You aren't disappointed that Kristi has decided to marry someone else?"

"Of course not, you little fool!" He shoved his hand into his pocket and withdrew a small black velvet box. He tossed it to her. "Here. I bought this a couple of weeks ago for you. I wanted to give it to you tonight."

Finley caught the box in trembling fingers and carefully opened the lid. Diamond and emerald earrings sparkled against the black velvet interior. "Bryan! Why, they match my necklace."

"Yes, I know."

Pulling her gaze from the jewels, she looked at Bryan and drew a deep breath. "Bryan, do you love me?"

A smile rested on his mouth, a smile that melted Finley's heart. "I'm not in the habit of marrying a woman I don't love, Red."

"But our marriage was just temporary," she reminded him.

"Maybe to you, not to me. Even though you acted indifferent to me, I suspected that you weren't. I asked your dad about it, and he assured me that you were just hiding your true feelings as a kind of defense." He shrugged and sat on the bed, his back to her. "In the short time we'd known each other, I'd fallen in love with you, but I knew you wouldn't believe it. I had this roving playboy reputation and I just knew you'd be too stubborn to believe me when I told you I was crazy for you. Your dad and I decided to use Kristi's vicious gossip as a means to get you to the altar. From there it was up to me to make you realize that we were meant for each other." He chuckled and shook his head, the light catching in the copper and blond strands of his hair. "It wasn't so easy, especially with people like Tanya shooting off their mouths."

Unable to keep the words back any longer, Finley whispered, "Bryan, I love you."

He had her in his arms before she finished the sentence and his lips took possession of hers in a kiss that told her all she needed to know. Pulling her with him, he lay on the bed, his mouth moving down the side of her neck and his hands exploring the curve of her breasts.

"Finley, Finley, you don't know how much I've wanted to hear you say that," he murmured, his lips brushing against the skin of her neck in a tantalizing way.

"I *have* said it," she told him, breathlessly.

"You have?" He lifted his head so that he could look down into her face. "When?"

"The night we—we made love. And today, on the field."

"I didn't hear you." He smiled and kissed the tip of her nose. "From now on, make sure I hear you say you love me. Okay?"

Finley smiled and nestled closer to him. "Sure you won't get tired of it?"

"Never," he said, drawing her closer to him so that she could feel his need of her.

"Bryan, your parents are waiting . . ."

"Let them wait a while longer," he murmured. "Once they see you, they'll understand why we're late. I do love you so, Finley."

Finley smiled and pulled his head down so that she could kiss him. Her lips parted beneath his and she vowed to never let him go. He was the captain of her heart.